# SILENT SHIELD

## SHIELDMAIDEN SQUADRON: BOOK THREE

## S.T. BENDE

*To my little Vikings.*
*And to everyone with the heart of a shieldmaiden.*

Silent Shield
Shieldmaiden Squadron: Book Three
Copyright © 2021, S.T. Bende
Edited by: CREATING ink
Cover Art by: Melissa Stevens of The Illustrated Author Design
Services
IBSN: 978-1-950238-19-4

First publication: 2021, S.T. Bende

Meet the faeries in

ALFHEIM ACADEMY

DARK FAERIE

ROYAL REBEL


Meet the demigods in NIGHT WAR SAGA.

PROTECTOR

DEFENDER

REDEEMER


*Complete list of S.T.'s licensed children's titles*

*at* https://www.stbende.com/kids-books/

"WE ARE GOING TO be in so much trouble," I hissed at my captain while hurriedly lacing my boots. Since discretion was of the essence at this ungodly hour, we'd kept the lights off—which meant our room was illuminated only by moonlight. This, coupled with my sheer exhaustion, had caused me to bump into the furniture more times than was becoming of a shieldmaiden. My eyes drifted to the digital clock on my nightstand, and I let out a soft groan. "We are well past curfew."

"Tell that to Torstein." Janna slid her sword into its sheath. "He's the one who asked for an assist."

"I'd help him with *anything*," Brigga said breathlessly.

Janna chuckled. "We know you would."

"Harumph." Brigga tied her blond hair back in a messy braid and pulled a few strands loose so they framed her face. After slicking on a coat of her new favorite lip gloss—the shiny pink one that smelled distinctly of strawberries—she pouted her lips and slipped her dagger into her belt. "I'm ready."

"Me too." Janna picked up her shield. She peered out the window of the sorority house. "Looks like Axel and Raynor are getting in the car. And Torstein's pacing on the sidewalk. We'd better hurry."

"How are we going to get out of here?" I slipped my own shield over my shoulder. "The second we open the front door we'll trigger the alarm and Lexi will be all over us. Again."

"That's why we're not going out that way." Janna unlatched the window. It gave off a delicate creak as she pulled it open with both hands. She stepped back, and motioned for me to come closer. "We'll take the alternate exit. Ingrid first, then Brigga. I'll bring up the rear."

Brigga arched one perfectly groomed brow. "You want us to climb down the side of Kappa Mu?"

"We've done worse."

Janna wasn't wrong. The cliffs we'd trained on back at the shieldmaiden compound on Valkyris were no joke. But a multimillion-dollar sorority house would be sorely lacking in crevices. And there was no ocean here to catch us if we fell.

I adjusted my sword and assessed my route. "Okay. The trellis to my right is covered in ivy, but I should be able to get a decent foothold. Brigga, wait for me to climb down. Then follow my path."

"Got it," Brigga said.

I slung one leg over the sill and slipped silently from the second-story window. My boots inched slowly along the narrow, white ledge as I shuffled carefully to the right. The trellis began two rooms over, which meant I'd have two solid chances of getting caught. But my team was counting on me . . . and I had no intention of letting anyone down.

A few weeks back, Brigga, Janna, Axel, Raynor, and I were sent one thousand years into the future to stop a dark mage from destroying our world. We were in a race to recover the ingredients he needed to enact a spell—one that, if successful, would enable Sverrir to *control mankind and all the realms.* Our mission wasn't going well. Sverrir currently had possession of three of the pieces he needed to control us all—illy bloom, meteor rock, and moonstone. Balboa bark was up for grabs, while we had a magical dagger, and eight of the world's twelve existing quanta crystals. Our light mage, Torstein, had just called in a trace on the ninth. Hence, our late-night sneak-out . . . and my precarious perch atop a sorority house drainpipe.

*Just. Don't. Fall.*

I swung around the pipe and reached over my shoulder to tug the hood of my sweater over my massive mane of crimson curls. Then I adjusted my fingerless gloves, lowered my head, and crept quietly along the ledge. I paused outside the first window, where soft snores slipped through the cracks. The evidence of my housemates' slumber unfurled the knot in my stomach. My fingernails dug into the windowsill as I placed one hand over the other. I was *so close* to the next ledge. I pointed my toe as I stretched outward, ignoring the burn in my thighs from my afternoon workout. My foot sought purchase on the wood. It slid into place and I clung like a starfish to the side of the structure.

Muffled guffaws rang up from the street. I turned my head with a growl. "Shut up, Axel!"

"Valkyris' finest," he called from the car.

"I am working!"

My boyfriend's quiet laughter echoed up the silent street.

"He is the worst," I muttered as I cleared the second window and latched onto the trellis. The boards were thin, but I kept my weight evenly distributed as I quickly climbed down the vine-laden wood. I'd just started to relax when my boot caught on a twisted branch and my toe slipped off the ledge. With a sharp inhale, I dug my fingers into the wood as I dangled outside the first-floor window. I tucked my knees to my chest, holding the tension in my arms while I struggled to steady myself. Axel's laughter triggered my last nerve. I cleared the final few feet with a stealthy jump.

When my boots hit the ground, I called quietly up to Brigga. "It's clear!"

Then I turned on one heel to give Axel a piece of my mind. "You are *not* helpful," I whispered as I stormed across the grass.

"And you are not graceful at two-thirty in the morning." He opened the door of the black-windowed car—an *SUV,* as Torstein called it. "I thought I taught you better than that."

I lifted my chin. "I didn't wake anyone up, did I?"

"No," Axel admitted. "Though Brigga sure might."

I turned to find Brigga dangling from the trellis. She squeaked delicately as she scrambled for a foothold. When she kicked the downstairs window, she earned a soft gasp from Janna.

"Careful," our captain called.

"I'm going to fall!" Brigga yelped.

And then she did. Her bird-like arms flailed as she plummeted to the ground.

"Brigga!" Raynor opened the other door and rushed from the car. "Are you hurt?"

"I'm fine." She untangled herself from the now-torn vines. "Let's just get out of here already."

"Please." Beside me, Torstein shook his head.

"Hey, guru." I greeted the light mage.

"Ingrid." Torstein nodded at me. "You *will* be on your game by the time we reach the beach, *ja?*"

"No promises." I shrugged. When he arched one brow, I caved. "Of course we will. We know what's on the line."

"Good." Torstein held the door as Brigga, Raynor, and I climbed in the back with Axel. Janna slipped into the front, while Torstein took his place in the driver's seat. "Because I've got a fairly strong read on another quanta crystal. And if we *hurry*"—he shot us a disdainful look in the mirror—"we can get it before Sverrir realizes it's there."

"Then what are you waiting for?" I fastened my seat belt. "Shieldmaiden Squadron—and guests. Move out."

The nearby village of Manhattan Beach was cloaked in darkness when Torstein parked along the deserted pier. Only the streetlamps illuminated its worn boards, red-roofed roundhouse, and sprinkling of empty benches. A handful of couples walked the vast expanse of sand, their silhouettes barely visible in the cloud-covered moonlight. We'd be able to slip in, claim the crystal, and return to campus before anyone was the wiser.

*I hope.*

"We're starting on the pier, right?" Axel pulled two broadswords from the back of the vehicle. He passed one to Raynor and gripped the other in his right hand.

"That was my original plan. But . . ." Torstein stepped out of the SUV. He held up his palms and turned slowly in a circle. Janna shot me a bemused look as we exited the vehicle, but neither of us spoke as the guru scanned the area for . . . whatever it was that told him when a bounty was nearby.

"The crystal is to the south," Torstein announced. He opened his eyes and pointed to his left. "I'm getting a pulse not too far from here—possibly on the sand, or a little way offshore."

"Anybody pack a swimsuit?" Raynor grinned.

"Let's go." Axel closed the door. He jogged for the

stairs leading down to the beach. I held tight to the strap of my shield as I ran after him. It was late enough that we shouldn't encounter any trouble. But preparation was nine-tenths of success.

And the dark mage was *not* to be underestimated.

"This way." Torstein hung a right. He ran closer to the water, using his hands to illuminate our path. His palms glowed, faint beams of light shooting from their surface. I had no doubt he was engaged in some magey sort of tracking, but if anyone caught sight of us, we'd be locked up for sure.

"Uh, Torstein?" I called. "Any chance you can put us in one of your magic bubbles? We look kind of suspicious."

"Of course." The mage directed one of his hand-beams overhead. A burst of light shot into the sky, splitting directly above Torstein before arcing into a dome. The shimmering surface glittered all around us —a transparent cage that added another degree of safety. We could see through it clearly, but it concealed us from curious eyes. *And hopefully dark mage ones, too.* "That better?"

"Much." I scanned the beach, looking for any sign of an enchanted crystal. "Are we close?"

"Feels like it." Torstein slowed to a brisk walk. I matched his pace as he trained his hand-beams on the line where the sea met the shore in a flutter of foamy waves. "I'm getting something this way—maybe thirty feet out?"

"I'll go in." Axel handed me his sword. He pulled his

shirt over his head, and threw it onto the sand. I tried not to stare at the twin rows of impressive abdominal muscles as he ran his hands over his man-bun and asked, "Is it a straight shot from here?"

"Yes," Torstein confirmed. "I don't know how deep the water gets, and you may have to search the ocean floor. Are you a strong swimmer?"

Axel smirked. "There's very little I'm *not* strong at."

There it was. The old Axel Andersson ego.

"Don't get caught in an undertow," I warned.

"Or eaten by a shark," Brigga added. "I read that those are common here."

"I'll be fine." Axel unlaced his boots. He kicked them off before marching across the sand. When he was waist deep in the water, he turned to face us. "If I'm not back in five minutes, send Raynor after me."

"Maybe I'd better go with him." Raynor was already untying his boots.

"Give him a chance." I staked the tip of Axel's sword in the sand. "He'll be impossible to deal with if he thinks we—oh! Axel, watch out!"

A massive wave crashed into my boyfriend. It dragged him under, pulling him from my view. Good gods, was he being sucked out to sea? My pulse spiked as I waited for him to surface. When he didn't immediately emerge, I threw down my weapons and ran for the water. "I'm going after him."

"Ingrid, stop! If the current isn't safe, there's nothing you'll be able to—"

I didn't hear the rest of Janna's warning. I charged

into the surf, the icy water chilling my flesh, and forcing a sharp inhale. The Pacific Ocean was even colder than I'd expected—nearly as cold as the North Sea in winter. But I didn't stop to dwell on the seemingly probable chance of losing a limb to frostbite. Axel still hadn't surfaced . . . and that wasn't good.

"Ingrid! Wait for me!" Raynor's hoarse cry hit me a second before I dove. The water nearly froze my eyelids shut, but I forced them open and scanned the murky sea.

*No sign of Axel.*

The saltwater stung my eyes but I ignored the burn as waves buffeted me from side to side. The motion left me nauseous, my gut churning like a barrel of butter. If this kept up, I was going to empty my stomach into the sea. But I couldn't give up—Axel was down there somewhere. And he needed my help.

I swam to the surface and filled my lungs with air. Then I brought my arms together, angled my body downward, and kicked. Axel was a strong swimmer. The fact that he hadn't surfaced meant something was seriously wrong. Maybe he'd hit his head, or a predator had struck. Anything was possible in unfamiliar waters. I swam as far as I could, stretching my arms in exaggerated strokes on the off chance I might catch an errant limb . . . or a tightly tied man-bun. The ocean was so vast, and the water so unsteady, my odds of finding him were slim to nonexistent. But they were even less with my eyes closed. Fighting against the pain, I forced my lids open and swept my head from side to side. All the while, I continued swimming downward, kicking as hard as I could and hoping I might catch Axel before he sank too deep. Because if he got swept out . . .

*Stop it, Ingrid. Just find him.*

*But what if I can't?*

I shook the thought from my head. Underwater panicking had never helped anyone. The only thing I could do was keep swimming . . . and keep searching. My eyes swept the area, scanning for any sign of Axel. But the effort was futile. Not only was the ocean too choppy, the moon must have fallen behind another cloud. Everything was pitch black. Everything . . . except a glowing, blue orb.

*What the actual Helheim?*

I clawed my way to the surface, and drew a deep breath. A quick scan of the waves revealed that Axel still hadn't emerged. But the orb seemed to be getting closer. It crept to the surface, floating upward like a slow-moving anglerfish. The creepy sea-creatures had been on the cover of my housemate Morgan's nature magazine, and I quickly scanned my memory, trying to remember whether the beast was poisonous . . . or carnivorous.

*Please, gods, don't let it be both.*

"Ingrid!" Raynor's voice came from my left. I whipped my head to find him swimming frantically toward me. "Are you all right?"

"I don't see Axel," I called back. "But there's definitely something down there. I think it's some kind of bioluminescent sea bea—augh!"

Something brushed against my leg. I kicked out.

"Stay still," Raynor warned. "If it senses movement, it may attack."

"I'm pretty sure it knows I'm here!" I yelled back.

I kicked again. The creature wrapped finger-like tentacles around my ankle.

"Oh my gods, it's got my foot!"

Panic seized my chest and I drove my heel into what I assumed was the sea beast's head. The pressure around my ankle released and I stroked toward the shore, trying to put as much space between us as I could.

"Raynor, clear out of here. I don't know how long that thing will—"

"Shieldmaiden!" Axel's ragged gasp paused my panicked paddling. "Are you trying to drown me?"

*Oh, thank gods. He's alive.*

Water dripped from Axel's beard as he reached out to steady me. His fingers wrapped firmly around my bicep, the touch warming my body despite the ocean's icy chill. When Axel released me, the strong curve of his shoulder lifted out of the sea and glinted in the moonlight. My eyes lingered on the thick, corded muscles that stretched along his arm.

"I'm glad you're okay," I panted. "But you'd better move it. There's some kind of sea beast with a bright biolumi—"

Axel raised his arm. He clutched a glowing, blue sphere.

"Oh. *Oh.*" Relief mixed with mortification. "I just attacked you, didn't I?"

"You did," Axel said good-naturedly.

"And you found the crystal?"

"Again, yes." Axel wiped a strand of kelp off his face. "What are you doing in the water?"

"She tried to save you," Raynor called. "When the water pulled you under, she thought you were a goner."

"We all did," I said defensively.

"Please." Axel flicked seawater at me. "It takes more than an ocean to bring me down."

"Yeah, well . . ." I treaded water. "Better safe than sorry, right?"

"Sure." Axel winked. He flipped onto his back and stroked toward the shore. "But I got what we came for, so can we please get out of this gods forsaken freezing water?"

"I thought you'd never ask." I swam for the sand, hoping we could all forget about the fact that I'd attacked the very person I'd been trying to save.

"You know, Shieldmaiden . . ." Axel swam alongside me. "We should do this more often. You look good soaking wet and fully clothed."

"Shut up, Axel," I said for the second time that night.

"Race you back."

"You'll never catch me." I put my face in the water and kicked hard. Each time I turned my head to breathe, Axel had gained a few inches on me. With a surge of adrenaline I lengthened my strokes, pulling until my arms struck the sand. I clamored to my feet and charged through the surf. Feet pounded behind me, but I ran as fast as I could, high-stepping my way to the shore and beating Axel in what was surely an impressive display of athleticism.

"Ingrid! Axel!" Janna's pitch was unnaturally high.

"It's okay." I doubled over, resting my forearms on my knees. "He's—*pant*—alive, and—*pant, pant*—I beat him. *Pant.*"

"Barely," Axel exhaled beside me. "And I got the crystal."

"I'm alive too," Raynor shouted from the water. "Thanks for asking."

"You all need to *get moving*," Janna yelled. "Torstein can't hold him off for much longer!"

My nerves pinged to attention. "Torstein can't hold *who* off?"

"Sverrir," Brigga said worriedly. "He's trying to breach the bubble."

Axel and I stared at each other, our competition instantly forgotten.

"Where is he?" I asked.

"There." Brigga pointed to the street. A white beam shot at the edge of Torstein's shield. It pinged off the protection, but a fissure had formed.

Axel pointed to the spot where our swords lay in the sand. Without a word, we launched across the beach and weaponed up.

"How long has he been here?" Raynor was right behind us.

"About two minutes." Janna already had her shield raised. "And the break has been steadily—oh, no."

A thunderous *crack* echoed across the beach. The white beam burst through the barrier, landing inside our bubble and launching a sandstorm that sent my team to its knees. I brought my shield up and shifted to my right, covering both Axel and myself beneath the wood. When the dust settled, I lifted my head. Sverrir leapt through the hole and landed on the sand.

And just like that, the whole game changed.

## CHAPTER 2

T HE DARK MAGE DIDN'T waste time. White beams soared across the beach, each landing closer to the spot where my team stood in a tight huddle.

"Don't let him anywhere near that crystal," I gritted out.

"Brigga. Take it." Axel passed over the stone. Brigga's eyes widened as she palmed the orb. Its glow had faded, but it continued to give off a faint light. That unwelcome beacon was going to be hard to hide.

"Torstein, can you do something about the light?" Brigga tucked the stone beneath her arm.

"Give me a minute." Torstein grunted. He lifted his hand and sent a blue beam barreling at Sverrir. The dark mage leapt lithely to the side. Torstein's brow furrowed into a deep *V*. He brought his hands together, whirled them in a tight circle, then pulled them apart to reveal a sparking, white orb between his palms. He glanced over his shoulder and called out, "Stay low. This might hurt."

I crouched down, inching closer to Axel. The assassin covered Brigga's body with his own. I positioned myself in front of him so all three of us were tucked behind my shield.

"We're secure," I yelled.

"I have Raynor," Janna called out.

"Good." Torstein lifted his hands over his head. A fierce cry ripped from his throat as he slammed the white orb into the earth. The ground shook, sending shockwaves ricocheting up my legs. My balance wavered and I tensed my muscles, fighting against the tremors that threatened to upend me. A massive wave broke against the shore, and the roundhouse at the end of the pier jiggled as if someone had shaken it. Torstein raised his hands and flung them forward. He seemed to be pushing something toward Sverrir. Whatever was happening, it made the tremors stronger. I squeezed the sand between my toes, desperately trying to steady myself against the force that rocked my balance. But I was no match for Torstein's handmade earthquake. I landed on the ground with a painful *thud*, sending a stabbing pain from the base of my tailbone all the way up my spine. My head whipped back, and I readied myself for a second jab—this one sure to knock me unconscious. But a steady hand stopped my trajectory, cradling the back of my skull just before it slammed into the ground.

"I've got you," Axel said.

I rolled my head to the side, careful to keep my shield aloft as I met Axel's emerald-green gaze. "Thanks."

"You okay?" he asked.

"Never better." I shifted to my hip, relieving some of the pressure from my freshly bruised backside.

*Ouch.*

"Guys." Brigga grunted. "I'm kind of squished."

Axel released my head. I rolled to one side. Another wave rocked the ground, and I climbed unsteadily to my knees.

"Stay behind me," I cautioned. "If Torstein's doing . . . whatever this is, then we can bet Sverrir's going to retali—oh, gods! Look out!"

A fiery sphere shot across the beach. It lit up the sky, casting an eerie glow as it made its way toward my team. I lifted my shield, knowing full well that if that fireball hit it, the wood would almost immediately be reduced to ash. But I wasn't going to be able to outrun fire—not with the ground rocking violently, and my legs seemingly reduced to wobbling sticks. I'd been in a mage battle recently, but that night on the Southern California State quad had been *nothing* like this. Back then, we'd been the ones to catch Sverrir off-guard. We'd had a strategy, and the element of surprise. Whereas tonight . . .

Things were *not* going well for Team Valkyris.

The fireball landed just a few feet from my shield. Its heatwave barreled toward me, and I flung my body over Brigga's, determined to protect our prize.

The crystal glowed bright beneath her arm. Its blue light was the last thing I saw before I squeezed my eyes shut and prayed the gods would spare me a death by flaming inferno. My Viking funeral wouldn't be nearly as meaningful if I showed up already burned to a crisp. Heat clawed at my back as I wrapped myself around my teammate, but before it could overtake me something hard and heavy pressed me to the ground. My shield was ripped from my hand as Axel took point. He must have placed himself between the blaze and my body, because the heat immediately dissipated . . . though the pressure only increased.

"Augh!" Brigga cried out. She was no doubt feeling crushed beneath the weight of two Valkyrians. But I didn't move for fear of exposing her to the fireball . . . and losing not only a teammate, but the prize we'd fought so hard to win.

"Blaze is out," Axel called. He rolled off of me, grabbing my forearm and helping me stand. He passed me my shield and quickly positioned himself in front of the still balled-up Brigga. "But he's just getting started."

"Keep Brigga guarded," Janna called out. "Raynor and I will block for Torstein. If Sverrir gets any closer we can break ranks and—"

Another fireball had her running toward our mage.

"Torstein, get behind me!" she shouted.

"No need." Torstein drew a spray of water from the ocean. He arched it into the air, directing it toward the fireball with his fingertips. When it hit the projectile, the flame morphed into a sea of raining sparks. Embers dropped onto the sand, hissing as they dissipated.

*What the actual Helheim?*

"I've got it," Torstein declared. "I've accessed the lineation of his spell, and conjured a counteraction that should—"

"No clue what that means, but Ingrid!" Axel swore. "Look out!"

"I'm on it." I darted toward the shape slithering to my left. *Where did that even come from?* A wide path through the sand suggested my newest assailant had been hiding in the dunes. But I didn't see it until it was nearly on top of me. Ignoring the nerves tumbling around my gut, I raised my sword and drove it into the massive snake. The blade pierced its belly, staking the sand in a single fierce strike. The creature writhed around, raising its head to bear its fangs at my exposed forearm. In my time as a shieldmaiden I'd battled warriors, dragons, and the not-quite-dead. But a venomous reptile in the middle of a California beach . . .

*How is this even possible?*

"Just. Die. Already." I punctuated each word by slamming my sword into the animal. It continued to come at me until I ripped my dagger from its sheath and swiped it parallel to the ground. It sliced through the snake's neck, cutting its head clean off and releasing the knot firmly clenched in my gut. "We're clear."

"We're not," Raynor called. "There's got to be half a

dozen snakes coming from the dunes. Where the Helheim is he getting these things?"

"We need to get out of here," Janna said. "Torstein, is there any chance you can get us to the car?"

"He already breached my shield." Torstein shot a blue beam toward the dark mage. "I'll try to bring up another protection, but I can't guarantee it'll hold long enough to get us out of here."

"This may help." Brigga held up the crystal. "It's been pulling toward you since Axel handed it to me."

"Mmm." Torstein shot another beam, then jogged over to Brigga. He took the blue stone from her hands, and cradled it between his fingers. "I wonder . . ."

He tightened his fist around the crystal. Then he closed his eyes, held up his other hand, and sent a stream of light straight into the air. It barreled a hundred feet upward, then split and arced its way to the ground. Light sparkled all around us, encasing us in a shimmering blue dome.

"Are we secure?" Axel asked.

"Only one way to tell." Torstein nodded toward the car. "I'll hold the protection—you all get to the car."

"Not so fast." I angled my sword at the snakes making their way toward my captain.

"I've got them," Janna confirmed. "Just get that crystal out of here."

A blast from the pier struck at the edge of the dome. Without a word, I backed toward Janna and sheathed my dagger. I drew my sword and pointed it at the approaching snakes. While the rest of our team ran for the car, Janna and I quickly disposed of the danger. Then, I scooped up my boots and followed my captain across the beach. Normally I would have found the sand between my toes to be soothing . . . but I was dripping wet, praying our magic crystal was safe, and ducking each time the evil sorcerer attacked our invisible bubble.

Gods, our life was weird.

Axel slowed his run, giving me time to catch up. He waved me forward and I jogged the short distance to the stairs. All the while, Sverrir kept up his assault. Light sparked on the pier side of the dome, but I kept my head down and ran. I cleared the stairs, followed Brigga and Raynor across the pavement, and threw myself into the back of the waiting vehicle. Axel jumped in after me. Torstein slipped into the driver's seat just as Janna flung open the passenger's door. When she'd closed it behind her, Torstein tossed her the crystal and started the car.

"Set the stone on the center console," Torstein ordered. "I'll keep a hand on it while I drive. If I can keep us shielded long enough, we can disappear in traffic and lose him."

"Well, drive fast." Axel peered out of the window. "He's coming up the stairs."

Janna swore loudly. She held out the crystal, and placed Torstein's right hand on top of it. "Drive, guru."

"Gladly." The tires screeched as Torstein pulled away from the curb. He glanced at the rearview mirror while he drove, occasionally releasing the crystal to fire a hand-beam out his window. My heart thundered against my ribs as we ran through stoplights and careened around corners. No doubt we would have attracted the wrong kind of attention during the daytime. But the clock on the dashboard read four-fifty-two, and save for the occasional car that quickly scooted out of our way, the streets of Manhattan Beach were mostly empty.

*Thank gods.*

Our light mage fired one more beam before rolling up his window, and returning both hands to the wheel.

"He's gone," Torstein said calmly. "Now, I know that your cover depends on returning to your residences, but it's a clear shot up this road to Malibu and I'd rather get this stone secured in my vault sooner than later."

"Just get that thing locked safely away." Axel slipped out of his soaking wet sweater. He dropped it at his feet, then leaned forward to study the glowing rock. "This puts nine of the twelve crystal pieces in our possession. *Ja?*"

"Correct." Torstein picked up speed as he merged onto Highway 1. "Raynor, there are towels in the far back—help yourself, and pass two up to Ingrid and Axel, would you?"

"Sure thing." Raynor reached behind him and grabbed three big, fluffy beach towels. He slung one around his shoulders, then handed the other two forward.

"Thanks." I tossed one of the towels to Axel. He

dabbed the droplets from his biceps while I began the tedious process of drying my abundance of curls. The saltwater had turned my hair to a tangled mess, so I finger-combed it as best I could before tying it back in a loose braid. I pulled off my sweater and towel-dried my arms, then did what I could to wring the water from my tank top. The cold hadn't bothered me when we were fighting, but now that I had some time to catch my breath . . .

I shivered. "Any chance you can turn up the heat?"

"Of course." Torstein pushed a button, and warm air filled the backseat. "And you're welcome to shower once we get to the Meditation Center. I've got plenty of dry yoga clothes lying around."

"I may take you up on that." My attention shifted to the still-glowing crystal. "I wonder how this one ended up in the ocean. You said your girlfriend hid them around Southern California—do you think she could have buried more of them at sea, or . . ."

"Ama was a gifted mage, but I doubt even she could breathe under water." Torstein shook his head. "Most likely, this one was buried on a nearby island. Over time, earthquakes or minor tsunamis could have unearthed it. It may have been adrift for years, for all we know. I only picked up on its whereabouts once it came close. The tides must have washed it in."

"Good thing," Brigga said. "If we'd been just a few minutes later, it would have fallen into the wrong hands."

"Sverrir was unusually quick to respond tonight."

Torstein frowned. "He didn't track us when we were in Palos Verdes—we were able to recover the previous two crystal pieces without his interference."

"*Ja.* The fire monster did the interfering for him." Axel reached over to rest his hand on my knee. I laced my fingers through his, pushing down the memory of the flaming beast who'd tried to stop us from collecting a pair of crystals in the forest two weeks ago. It had been an absolutely horrific day. The attack had been so vicious—and my boyfriend so badly hit—that for a few terror-filled minutes I'd been convinced I was going to lose Axel forever. That fear blossomed anew tonight, when he didn't emerge from the water. And while I understood that loss was just a part of the package in our line of work, it wasn't easy to know that on any given mission, at any given moment, my boyfriend could be incapacitated. *Or worse.*

I squeezed Axel's hand. "We'd better be on our guard the next time Torstein gets a read on a stone. We got off lucky tonight—we didn't have to go head-to-head with a fiery monster *or* a maniacal mage. We just had to dodge a few fireballs."

"And snakes." Janna shook her head. "What was that about? He can control *snakes?*"

"Animal manipulation is an advanced dark practice." Torstein scowled. "I was unaware that he had that ability."

"Yeah, well, now we know," Axel said. "So let's stay away from barns."

"And the zoo," Raynor said drily. "I read that they

keep *polar bears* there. Can you imagine what he could do if he got a hold of one of those?"

"Or wildcats," Brigga whispered. "I read they had those, too."

"How about we just steer clear of all carnivorous animals?" Axel said easily. "And let's get this crystal locked away, so we can get back to our boring, collegiate lives."

"Yours may be boring." Brigga snorted. "The three of us are in for an earful if Lexi finds out we've been gone all night."

"Luckily, she's too lazy for Friday morning classes," I pointed out. "So long as we make it back in time to catch Morgan on her way to folklore, we'll be fine."

"We're nearly to my compound." Torstein steered the vehicle off the highway, and up a steep hill. "It shouldn't take long to get this secured, and then I can drop you all off."

"Sounds good." Axel leaned back in his seat.

We drove the rest of the way in silence. When we turned into the renowned Spiritual Center for Meditation, I released my hold on Axel's hand. My pulse quickened as I peered out the window. "There are cars here?"

"Of course," Torstein said calmly. "Sunrise meditation begins in half an hour."

"Right." I'd forgotten about the practicalities of Torstein's *serenity now* empire.

"No need to worry. Nobody will see the crystal," Torstein assured us. "I'll park around the back."

He drove past the main building toward the north end of the campus. This side of the compound was home to a collection of bungalows and Torstein's underground vault—the one currently holding a gaggle of energetically enhanced quanta crystals. He parked in a small garage, then ushered us into the attached bungalow.

"This is my place," he said. "I've got two full bathrooms so Ingrid, Axel, Raynor—feel free to shower and change. Towels are in the hall closet, and my bedroom's back there." He pointed. "You'll find yoga clothes in the bottom drawer of my dresser—help yourselves to whatever fits."

"Thanks," I said gratefully. My bare arms were still covered in goose bumps.

"Janna and Brigga, why don't you come with me? It never hurts to have backup. Once we get the crystal into the vault, I'll drive you all home."

"Sounds like a plan," Janna said.

"I've been wanting to see your vault," Brigga admitted. "Is it true the crystals *sing* when they're together?"

Torstein arched his brow at me.

"What? It's *really* weird." I shrugged. "I had to tell somebody."

"Yes, they sing." Torstein smiled. "Come on. I'll show you."

The three of them headed outside. I went into Torstein's room and raided his drawer for clothes, while Raynor pulled fresh towels out of the closet.

"You two can go first," he offered when I came out. "I'll take the next open shower."

"Thanks, Raynor." I traded him sweats and a T-shirt for a thick, white towel. Then I tossed a second set of workout clothes to Axel. "These are for you. See you guys when I'm *not* covered in saltwater."

"But it's such a good look on you," Axel teased.

"Isn't it though?" I winked.

I retreated to one of the bathrooms, intent on warming my goose-pimpled flesh with a gloriously hot shower. I'd have much preferred a bath—an hour-long soak in a bubble-filled tub would have been absolute heaven. But after the night I'd had, I had little doubt that this shower would be among the most exquisite experiences of my entire week.

I only wished it could have lasted longer.

## CHAPTER 3

THANKS TO LOS ANGELES' all-too-predictable traffic, Torstein pulled up to fraternity and sorority row just minutes before we had to leave for class. Axel and Raynor leapt from the SUV and ran across the empty lawn of the Alpha mansion. Most of their housemates preferred to sleep in on Fridays, which made sneaking inside pretty easy for them. Whereas at the Kappa Mu house . . .

"Why are there so many people?" Brigga leaned over my shoulder. She pointed out the darkened window, counting the unusually large number of girls gathered on the porch. "It's normally just us, Morgan, and a handful of freshmen on Friday mornings."

"They're all pledges," Janna observed. "Maybe they had some kind of event."

"Maybe," I said. "Whatever it is, we need a cover story. Uh . . ." I drummed my fingertips on my sheathed sword. "We're dressed for combat, so theatre rehearsal?"

"Aren't those usually *after* school?" Brigga frowned. "We're also in a car, so early morning coffee run?"

"With swords?" Janna shook her head.

"Besides, they have coffee in the house. Maybe we—oh!" I jumped as a tight fist rapped on Janna's window. The serene face of our sorority sister/resident yoga instructor, Kenzi Takahashi, peered through the glass. She tucked a strand of glossy, black hair behind her ear as she motioned for Janna to roll the window down.

"What's that story, now?" Brigga hissed.

"Shh." Janna forced a smile on her face as she lowered the glass. "Good morning, Kenzi."

"There you are!" The beads on Kenzi's caftan clicked as she stepped back onto the grass. "I was worried when you didn't come to yoga, but it looks like you had another meditation class today. Morning, Torstein."

Ah, there it was. Our cover story. *Thank you, Kenzi.*

"Hello." The guru folded his hands together in prayer. He bowed his head so his long, blond hair fell over his face. When he looked back up, his sky-blue eyes twinkled. "Yes, we were doing a special session together. Because today marks an ancient Norwegian nature ritual, and it's important to honor our ancestors."

I snuck a look at Janna. Was that true?

She shrugged as she opened the car door.

"Ooh." Kenzi nodded. "It's vital that we pay respect

to the souls who have paved the way so that we may follow our unique path of incarnation."

I glanced at Brigga as we climbed out of the car. Sometimes I had no idea what Kenzi and Torstein were talking about.

"I apologize for keeping them so long. I didn't realize you have a standing yoga session." Torstein smiled ruefully. "Perhaps I can make it up to you with a private meditation. What are you doing now?"

Kenzi's face lit up. "I don't have class until noon."

"Great. Hop on in." Torstein motioned to the now-empty passenger seat. Kenzi climbed inside, and gave the guru a beatific smile. She'd once told us that one-on-ones with the world-renowned spiritual coach were rare—and *highly* sought after. I wasn't sure if she had a crush, or just really admired his . . . enlightenment. Either way, her smile lit the entire street as she and Torstein drove away, headed off to discover their inner peace.

*Or something.*

"Well, that was easy." Janna walked toward the throng of pledges. She raised her voice as she said, "Good thing our *morning meditation class* is over in time for school!"

"Yes," I agreed loudly. "It's always nice to start the day with a *meditation class.*"

"You bring *that* to meditate?" One of the pledges stared at my shield.

"It was a heritage meditation," Brigga said quickly. "Honoring our ancestors."

"Oh, right. Because you're exchange students." Another pledge nodded. "I'll bet you miss . . . Sweden?"

"Norway," Brigga corrected. "And yes. We do."

"More than you know," I muttered.

"We'd better get going," Janna said. "We don't want to be late for class."

"Of course," one pledge said as she stepped to the side, clearing the path to the door.

I followed Janna and Brigga upstairs and quickly changed out of my borrowed sweats into something more suitable for a morning class at So Cal State. The students here were *very particular* about their clothes—at least, the female students were. The males seemed to throw on whatever was comfortable. I was only mildly jealous.

When I was dressed, I appraised my outfit with a sigh. "I will never understand their folk costumes."

"What? Mini-skirts and tight sweaters aren't your favorite look?" Brigga twirled in front of the full-length mirror. She'd swapped her combat gear for a short, flared skirt and a top that left very little to the imagination. The entire ensemble was in what the girls here called "winter white."

Whatever that was.

"No. They're not." I tugged the hem of my black skater skirt and adjusted the tie on my ballet sweater. The last few weeks had been a crash course in fashion words. Though, to be fair, learning that had been a lot easier than learning to swordfight with Axel without killing him.

31

"Hustle, ladies," Janna said. "I just saw Morgan go downstairs. You know how she feels about being late."

"Better hurry then." Brigga handed me a notebook. "Class starts in twenty minutes. This week's lecture is on local legends."

"How do you remember so much?" I slipped the notebook into the satchel hanging from my desk chair. Then I snuck a quick glance in the mirror. My freckled face was even paler than usual, so I pinched my cheeks to give them a flush of color.

"I'm the disseminator. It's my *job* to procure and distribute information." Brigga rolled her eyes. "Besides, you're too busy training with Axel to stay on top of our homework assignments."

"I pull my academic weight here just fine, thank you very much." I shouldered my bag and tossed my crimson curls over one shoulder. "Besides, someone has to protect our butts in the field."

"*Someones,*" Janna corrected. She dusted a coat of blush over her cheeks, giving her cocoa-hued skin a rosy glow. Then she smoothed the front of her dress and grabbed her own pack. A piece of paper fell out, and I bent to pick it up.

"What's this?"

"Hmm? Oh, good find. It's my notes on the map we found in Sverrir's camp. I was brainstorming during astronomy class and—"

"The planetary alignment is in two weeks." I traced my finger along the page. "His map predicts the energy will funnel to somewhere just south of here. In . . . San Diego?"

Brigga stopped combing her hair. "Our winter formal is in San Diego."

"What are the odds," I said drily.

"We don't have time for that now." Janna retrieved the paper from my hand. She slid it into her desk drawer and walked through the bedroom door. "Everybody, downstairs. We don't want Morgan asking questions."

"Morgan always asks questions," I mumbled. I plastered a smile on my face and followed my teammates to the first floor. When we reached the dining room, Morgan looked up from the coffee cart with a smile.

"There you are! I was just about to come and check on you." She raised a travel mug to her lips and took a drink. "Are you ready for Folklore?"

"Almost." I quickly poured some coffee into a takeaway cup and attached its lid. "Okay, now."

Janna furrowed her brow. "You actually like that stuff?"

"Not at all," I admitted. "But it works."

Janna picked up her own cup and filled it. "Fair enough. Brigga? Want some?"

Brigga wrinkled her nose. "I'll pass."

I shrugged. "Suit yourself."

The four of us walked outside. Raynor and Axel stood on the sidewalk, both with their arms folded across their chests. They'd swapped their borrowed clothes for the athletic pants and hoodies their fraternity brothers wore to classes. I was momentarily distracted by the loose waves that framed Axel's thick beard—he usually kept his hair pulled back in a man-bun. But it wasn't long before my eyes zeroed in on the twin sets of yoga pants and cropped tops standing in front of our teammates. Lexi and Becky, my nemesis and her second-in-command, faced Axel and Raynor with their chests pushed forward. They alternated flirty hair tosses with hands-on-hips "I'm listening" poses, and though their backs were to me I could clearly see that they were on the hunt. Lexi'd had her eye on Axel since the day we dropped into Los Angeles. And because she was exceptionally thick-headed, she couldn't process that Axel was *my* boyfriend. Even if his eyes did linger on her bare midriff for a few seconds longer than was absolutely necessary.

Irritation nudged at my gut. Why was Axel even—

"What are they doing up?" Janna grimaced.

"You know Lexi would never miss a chance to torture us." I rolled my eyes.

"Do you think she knows we snuck out?" Brigga wrung her hands together.

"Torstein covered for us," I reminded her. "And if you think she's into Axel, just *wait* until she catches sight of Mister Tall, Blonde, and . . . what did you call him? Gods-level-gorgeous?"

"Shh." Brigga swatted me. "Raynor will hear you."

"What will I hear?" Raynor stepped to the side and grinned at Brigga.

Lexi turned around with a scowl. "We were talking."

"And now we're walking," Morgan called from down the sidewalk. She waved the boys toward her. "Sixteen minutes until Folklore."

"Of course." Raynor nodded. "Becky. Lexi. Have a good morning."

"You'll let us know?" Lexi twirled her hair around one finger. She batted her lashes. "You know, about our offer?"

"I don't think that it's the best idea." Axel reached out and rested his fingertips on Lexi's shoulder. Every nerve in my body pinged with irritation.

*Why is he touching her?*

"Just *think* about it," Lexi wheedled.

"Think about what?" I stepped forward so I stood closer Axel.

"Please." Lexi kept her focus on my boyfriend. Whose hand *still* had not left Lexi's arm.

*What the actual Helheim, Axel?*

"Look, we appreciate it," he said. His fingertips tightened around her shoulder. Lexi practically purred.

My irritation jumped to anger. "What do you appreciate?"

Axel turned to me with an easy smile. Apparently, he was oblivious to his tremendous display of idiocy.

*Typical.*

"I appreciate Lexi's invitation to, uh . . ." His eyes glazed over as Lexi pulled her shoulders back and stuck out her chest.

"Her invitation to what?" I prompted through gritted teeth.

"Huh? Oh. To present the seniors at the winter formal." Axel's gaze slowly shifted from Lexi's cleavage to my clenched jaw. "Hey, you okay? You look tense."

*I swear to gods, I am going to kill him.*

Raynor chimed in just as I balled my fists. "What Axel's trying to say is that as honored as we are, we have to decline. The terms aren't agreeable given our situation."

"What are the terms?" I drew my elbow back. I still hadn't ruled out clocking Axel in his insanely square jaw.

"Just *think* on it, mmm? It would make the formal so . . . perfect." Lexi ran one finger along Axel's considerable bicep. "Well, we'll see you around."

"See you." Axel shot Lexi a goofy smile before sauntering to my side. "Hey, you," he said as if nothing had happened.

*That's it. I'm punching him.*

He tilted his head and stared at me. "You really do look tense. Anything wrong?"

A low growl built in my throat. If Axel thought it was okay to flirt with other girls—especially really awful ones—in front of me, then maybe we weren't where I thought we were.

I turned on my heel and stormed down the sidewalk.

"Ingrid!" Axel's footsteps pounded behind me. "Are you mad?"

"Are you *seriously* asking that?" I took a furious drag

on my coffee. Hot liquid splashed down my throat, and I sputtered.

"Come on, Shieldmaiden," he pleaded. I shirked his hand off my shoulder. "Just talk to me."

"Wouldn't you rather be talking to Lexi?" I didn't slow my stride.

"Not particularly." He fell in step beside me. Janna, Brigga, and Raynor kept a safe distance.

"Oh, no?" I glared at him. "Because your focus seemed pretty clear."

On her prominently displayed chest.

*Grr.*

"Well, *ja.*" Axel looked confused. "I *was* clear that I wouldn't be her date to the formal."

My cup slipped from my hand. Axel's hand snaked out to catch it before I dropped my coffee all over my shoes.

"Can I have some?" He didn't wait for an answer before lifting the cup to his pale, perfect lips. "Mmm. This is good stuff."

"Lexi asked you to the winter formal?" I balked.

"Well, technically she asked if Raynor and I would present the seniors." Axel took another drink. "What she didn't mention until *later* was that we'd have to be her and Becky's dates to do it."

My eyes narrowed to slits. "What do you mean, *later*? How long were you talking to her?"

Axel took one more sip before passing the cup back to me. "I don't know. Why? You jealous, Shieldmaiden?"

I tossed my hair. "Ha. You wish."

"Aw, don't be like that." He slung an arm around my shoulders and led us down the sidewalk. "You know you're the only girl for me."

"Didn't look like it," I muttered.

"I was just maintaining our cover." He leaned in to brush a series of feather-light kisses along my neck. Goose bumps broke out across my skin as his tongue moved slowly up to my ear. Gods, he was good at this.

"*Ja.* Well . . ." I reluctantly leaned away. "Just remember this *cover* will end. Lexi's not going home with us."

"Good." Axel leaned in again. "Now, how can I make you less mad? I know. What if I—"

I cupped his beard in my hand. "We have to get to class. We're going to give poor Morgan a heart attack."

I turned Axel's face forward.

His brow furrowed as he stared at Morgan speed-walking ahead of us. "Talk about tense . . ."

I shrugged. "Helheim hath no fury like a girl we've nearly made late for class. Again."

"Is it safe to approach?" Janna came up beside me. "Or are you still debating ripping Axel's head off?"

I smirked at my captain. "How'd you know?"

"Lucky guess." She mimed a balled fist.

"Axel can live . . . for now." I let him lace his fingers through mine as we walked toward campus. "But who knows what tomorrow holds?"

"That's the fun of dating me," Axel said confidently. "You just never know what surprises are in store."

Janna shook her head. "Did you and Raynor run into any trouble back at your house?"

"We don't have curfews, if that's what you're asking." Axel grinned. "Nobody even noticed we were gone."

"Lucky," I muttered.

"I'm just going to go ahead," Morgan yelled over her shoulder. "I'll see you there!"

Janna sipped at her coffee. "Blech, I don't know how you drink this stuff."

Axel's eyes widened. "I'll take yours."

"Suit yourself." Janna passed him the cup. "I miss tea."

"They have tea here," I pointed out.

"Not the kind we have back home. Here, everything's sweet or flowery or *herbal*, which seems like a pretty loose interpretation, if you ask me. Since when is a lemon an herb?" Janna sighed. "Oh, well. We'd better catch up to Morgan. No point stressing her more than we already do."

She jogged the ever-growing distance between us and our housemate. Axel and I took a few more sips of our coffee, then tossed the containers in a bin and picked up our pace. We entered the folklore classroom with a full minute to spare.

"See, Morgan?" Axel reached down the row to pat Morgan's still-tensed shoulder. "Nothing to worry about."

"Mm-hmm." Morgan was too busy lining up her notebook, textbook, and extra pencils to look up.

We really had to stop making her life harder.

"Welcome, students. I see nearly *half* of you have decided to come to class today. So gold stars to each of you." A bemused Professor Clark took his place at the front of the classroom. He smiled at us from behind too-big eyeglasses that made his kindly face look a bit like an owl's. Professor Clark was one of those teachers who truly cared about his students. He often incorporated stories from his own life into his lectures, and as he sipped at the water glass he always kept at his podium, I wondered what personal examples he might bring to today's lesson on . . . I glanced at the smartboard in the front of the classroom.

*Local Legends: Real Life Ghost Stories from the So Cal Region.*

"Professor." A girl in the front row raised her hand. "Nobody from Southern California calls it *So Cal.*"

"Well, I'm from Minnesota." Professor Clark smiled. "So I've proven your point, Miss Carlson."

The girl and her seatmates laughed.

"Now, if you're done critiquing my lecture titles . . ." Professor Clark adjusted his glasses. "Let's jump in, shall we? My husband and I spent last weekend at a charming hotel in San Diego. A quaint little place— perhaps you've heard of it. The Hotel Del Coronado?"

He clicked his remote, and the title behind him slid off the screen. It was replaced by a picture of a grand castle—one with white walls and red roofs, and taking up what looked to be at least four full dragon barns' worth of land.

"Did the meaning of 'quaint' change in the last thousand years?" I whispered to Janna.

She glanced to her right where Morgan frantically took notes.

"I think that was sarcasm," Janna whispered back.

*Ah.*

"Now, there are many stories of ghost sightings throughout this region. The Hollywood Roosevelt Hotel is believed to be haunted by a trumpet-playing actor who roams the halls of the ninth floor. And, of course, its most famous resident is rumored to make appearances in the mirror of her old suite."

"Marilyn Monroe," offered a boy in the back.

"One and the same." Professor Clark smiled. "She's also said to have been spotted at the Hotel Del. As you know, my husband Kevin is *quite* the fan. He was hoping we might run into her, so to speak, during our stay. Alas, our visit was specter-free. Though we *did* get an earful from the staff about the infamous ghost that haunts room three thousand three hundred and twenty-seven. And this made me wonder . . . from the Queen Mary to the Roosevelt to the Hotel Del, it seems Southern California is ripe with ghost stories. So how did it come to be that way? Where did all of this *magic* originate?"

Professor Clark clicked again. A black-and-white image of a field replaced the opulent hotel.

"Once upon a time, in a land not too far from where Kevin and I spent the weekend, a vast field overlooked an undeveloped area. In what came to be known as

Balboa Park, a variety of shrubs, roots, and herbs grew uninhibited. One such shrub grew wilder than the others. Locals called it *balboa* and believed its bark to have mystical properties. Under the full moon, it was believed to shed its skin and join with the community of elementals—the fairies, air spirits, and water gnomes that made up the tapestry of the *otherworld*. The bark it left behind was said to contain the magic of all the creatures it met along its journey . . . and it was prized for its ability to cure sickness, produce riches, and even reverse aging."

My lips formed a small *O. Balboa* bark. What were the odds?

Morgan raised her hand. "Like an herbal fountain of youth?"

"There's that word again," Janna whispered. "Herbal."

"Just get on board with coffee," I whispered back.

Brigga leaned over Axel to grasp my hand. "Oh my gods! Balboa bark. Like in Sverrir's spell."

I nodded silently.

"Yes, Morgan. It *was* said to be like a fountain of youth." Professor Clark nodded at Morgan while I locked eyes with Brigga. Axel stroked his beard, no doubt wondering the same thing as me. Could our teacher lead us to the location of one of the dark mage's last remaining ingredients?

Axel raised his hand.

"Yes, Mister . . ." Professor Clark tilted his head. "I'm

sorry, I don't recall your name. You've not come to my office before."

"I'm Axel Andersson," Axel said easily. "Professor, where did you say this bark was located?"

"In Balboa Park, ironically." The teacher chuckled. "Though I assure you, Mr. Andersson, the balboa bark *does not* have the magical properties legends prescribe to it. This is, after all, a *folklore* class."

"Why do you say ironically?" Brigga asked.

"Because the park wasn't named for the mystical plant. It was actually named long after the legend of the bark originated. It was named for a European explorer —Vasco Nuñez de Balboa, who first sighted the Pacific Ocean during his expedition in Panama. Write that down—it *will* be on your exam."

Morgan scribbled furiously.

"It's pure coincidence that the legendary tree/shrub/root—the stories aren't entirely clear, and nobody's ever actually *found* the balboa, seeing as it is *mere legend*—bears the same name. Though, of course, it's entirely possible that the explorer was chosen as the park's namesake because of the similarities in nomen-clature."

"That means *how names are chosen*," Brigga said slowly to Axel.

"I know what it means." He rolled his eyes.

"Did you?" I whispered.

"Maybe," he whispered back.

*Snort.*

"I guess we know where we're heading next," Brigga whispered.

"Unless Sverrir's already cleared the place out." I glanced at Janna. "Remember the illy flower?"

"Do I ever." She groaned.

"Shh," Morgan hissed. "The professor is talking!"

"Right. Sorry." Janna shot us a look, and we all fell silent. Sure enough, Professor Clark had moved on— this time, the image on the screen was one of a massive, metal boat. The words *Queen Mary* were inscribed on its side.

I turned the page of my notebook and jotted a few words. Then I slipped the book into Axel's hand. A minute later, he passed it back.

*Good idea,* he'd written. *Let's run it by him.*

I nodded. Then I closed the notebook and laced my fingers through Axel's. His thumb ran slow circles over the back of my hand, and I tried to focus on the tingles he sent up my arm instead of the nerves pinging around in my gut. But I couldn't shake the worry that had built inside of me. We were always one step behind the dark mage. And if Sverrir had already found the allegedly nonexistent balboa bark . . . our crystals and Freia's dagger might just be the only things preventing him from destroying our world.

*Dritt.*

## CHAPTER 4

T HE NEXT DAY, AXEL, Janna, and I sat around a small conference table at Torstein's Spiritual Center for Meditation. We'd gathered in a bungalow in the north compound—one next door to Torstein's residence, and a few buildings over from one that concealed his underground vault. Raynor and Brigga had stayed behind—they'd be hitting the library to research the possibly mythical balboa while the rest of us worked out our plan of attack. We needed to determine whether Torstein could get a read on the local legendary plant . . . and whether we could take it out of play entirely.

"I talked to Professor Clark after class." Janna rested her forearms on the pale, oak tabletop of the makeshift conference room. An untouched mug of tea steamed beside her. "The stories say that the balboa is *one* plant —not an entire grove. So if it's moveable, we may be able to dig it up and bring it to a safe location. If it's small enough, we could hide it in the vault."

"Except that if it does exist, which is still in question, it's likely to be a protected plant." Torstein frowned. "Environmental regulations are fairly strict in this region. If there really is only one of this thing, whether they've identified it as balboa or otherwise, they're going to have all kinds of laws against removing it—or even touching it, most likely."

"Since when have we let *the law* stop us?" Axel stretched his arms overhead.

"Since we needed to *not* get arrested, locked up, and taken out of commission. We can't give Sverrir a clear path to those final ingredients." Janna shook her head.

"We're the only people currently alive who know what he's up to." I sighed. "Which makes us the only ones with the power to stop him. We have to make sure we do it right."

Axel ran his palms over his man-bun. "So how exactly do we do that?"

Torstein stared out the window. "I'm not entirely sure," he admitted.

"Can you get a read on the plant?" I asked. "Pick up on its vibration or something, like you did with the crystals? It's rumored to be in Balboa Park, but if nobody's ever found it, well . . . we have no reason to believe it's actually there."

"I can try," Torstein said. "Usually I'd need a sample —something I could feel a pulse from. But if it is real, and if it's truly enchanted, it will have a different resonance from the other organic matter in the region. I can follow the aberration and possibly locate the plant."

"Great." Janna nodded.

"What's odd is that I'd never heard of it before I met all of you." Torstein tapped his fingertips against his mug. "So far as I know, it wasn't in existence during the mage war, which means this *Control* spell must have come into existence sometime after our crystals were charged."

"Either that, or it was such a huge secret, nobody in Norway had ever heard of it." I glanced at Axel. "Were there mages in this part of the world back then? Or now?"

"I'm not sure." Torstein raised his mug to his lips. He took a slow drink. "We coordinated our efforts during the war, but we limited our conversations to the task at hand. Our safety had always depended on operating mostly in secret."

"Why?" Janna asked.

"Back then, the world was ruled by kings and queens—most of whom were willing to kill to have a mage in their court. And very few of those monarchs wanted to use our abilities for the greater good. Once we eliminated the threat of a super-charged crystal falling into dark hands, the danger of remaining together was too great."

"So you split up," Axel deduced.

"Correct." Torstein set his mug on the table. "And in all these years, I've never encountered a balboa."

"Well, hopefully we'll encounter one soon," I said.

"Encounter . . . and procure." Axel drummed his fingers on the table. "If Torstein does manage to track it, we have to bring it in. Secure it in the vault, so Sverrir can't get his hands on—"

"Shh." Torstein held up one finger. "Do you feel that?"

"Feel what?" Axel glanced at me. I shrugged.

"That . . . push." Torstein stood. He walked around the table to stare out the window.

"I don't feel anything," Janna said uneasily.

"Me neither." Axel's eyes shifted to the table by the door. Since Torstein's compound was protected, we'd checked our weapons when we came in.

An uneasy wave rippled through me. It swirled around my gut before seeping up to my chest. *Oh, no.* "What is it?"

"I'm . . . not sure." Torstein opened the window and leaned outside. A crisp, sea breeze swept into the room. The salty tang reminded me of home, the smell of the Pacific nearly identical to that of the North Sea. But this was no time for reminiscing. Torstein's shoulders pulled back, and the vein across his jaw bulged. He was on high alert.

"Torstein?" I said quietly. "What's going on?"

"There's something here . . ." Long, blond hair fell over one shoulder as he turned his head to peer around the bungalow. "I can't see it but . . . oh, gods."

"What?" Axel's chair clattered to the floor. He jumped to his feet and raced toward the weapons table.

"An intruder." Torstein's hands sparked. A shimmering, blue orb fired up between them.

Axel swore. He tossed me my sword before picking up his own. I snatched the blade from the air, then ran to retrieve my shield.

"Location?" Janna barked.

"Mountain side of the bungalow compound." Torstein closed his eyes. "It's a malignant presence of unknown origin."

"What does it want?" I opened the front door. Janna and Axel thundered outside.

"I have no idea." Torstein met my gaze with a wide-eyed stare. "But we're about to find out."

"Ingrid," Axel yelled from. "You'd better get out here."

I nodded at Torstein before running through the doorway. His footsteps pounded behind me as I made my way along the cobblestone path winding between one-story buildings. I didn't stop until I'd found Axel and Janna. They'd both dropped to a fighting stance. Their weapons were pointed at a thick, black stream.

Torstein growled quietly.

"What the Helheim is that thing?" Axel called over his shoulder.

I raised my shield and fell in beside him. "Nothing good, that's for sure."

"I thought this place was protected." Janna lifted her shield.

"It is," Torstein said. "This is unprecedented."

I narrowed my eyes. "Why is everything with us 'unprecedented?'"

"Because we're tough, Shieldmaiden." Axel didn't look away from the stream. "Wouldn't want life to get boring, now would we?"

Gods, no. That would be awful.

"Look out!" Janna shouted.

The stream darted forward. It struck like a snake, its black smoke soaring across the path in a swift jab. Axel leapt in front of it. His grunt was punctuated by the woosh of his slashing sword. The darkness promptly dissipated. It evaporated into the ether as if it had never even existed.

*I don't trust it.*

Axel didn't retreat. "Did I get it?"

Torstein moved alongside Axel. He transferred his blue orb to one hand. With the other, he reached out to touch the spot where the smoke had been. Black light sparked from his fingertips. He quickly withdrew his hand. "It's still there."

"So what do we do?"

"I think we—augh!" Axel's torso lurched to one side as if he'd been pushed. Whatever this thing was, it was *strong*.

And we couldn't even see it coming.

Axel stumbled a second time, then quickly regained his footing before driving his sword into the invisible intruder. Black sparks shot through the air. The smoke-snake swiftly reformed. It wrapped itself around Axel, picked him up, and flung him onto the grass. While the assassin scrambled to his feet, Janna and I moved forward. We kept our shields at the ready while we jabbed our swords at our attacker. What appeared as little more than ashy air packed a surprisingly strong punch. Each jab was returned with a fierce wrench, pulling me off-balance and nearly forcing my arm out of its socket. I struck again, this time eliciting a shower of sparks. They sprayed off the metal of my blade in a blazing hot waterfall. Was this smoke somehow filing our swords? Could it actually destroy our weapons?

"Fall back!" Janna ordered. "Torstein, this isn't working."

"I see that." The mage lowered his head. He brought his hands together, charging his orb before throwing it into the stream. The darkness recoiled, pulling back like a wounded snake. But seconds later it was on the move. It pushed Torstein and threw him to the ground next to Axel.

"Janna!" I shouted.

"On it." My captain was already running. The two of us raced after the smoke, following its serpentine movements along the cobblestones and toward the cliff. As it rounded the corner, I launched myself into the air. With my shield in front of my chest, I drew my arm back and angled my sword down. I'd set myself up to land on top of our assailant—and hopefully, to drive my Valkyrian blade through whatever vital organs it possessed. It might have been able to protect itself on the outside, but hopefully here, in its center, it would—

"Augh!" My blade struck an invisible wall. The impact reverberated up my arm, rocking my bones to their very core. The pressure built in my wrist until I released my grip on my sword. It flew in the air as I dropped to the ground.

My shoulder struck the cobblestones with a painful crack. Pain shot up my neck, and I rolled my head to one side as my blade glinted overhead. It spiraled downward in a terrifyingly fast trajectory. I was about to be impaled by my own weapon! My arm moved instinctively, lifting my shield to cover my body. The world around me slowed to a standstill as I curled into a ball and prayed that the sword wouldn't pierce my protection.

This was *not* how I wanted to die.

*Thwack!*

The clang of metal on metal was followed by a resounding thump. Footsteps pounded just beside my head, and a warm hand reached down to pull me up. "Come on, Shieldmaiden. You've got to move."

"Axel!" I blinked at my avenging assassin. "What did—"

"I knocked your blade into the next lawn." He pointed with his broadsword. "It was about to do you wrong. So I—"

"Thanks." I ran across the grass and retrieved my wayward weapon. When I turned around, our assailant —and our teammates—were gone. *"Dritt!"*

"Janna and Torstein are fine—they're fighting the stream." Axel jogged toward the cliff. I adjusted my shield and ran after him. "But it's winding between the bungalows. We aren't sure where it's—"

"The vault!" Torstein's cry echoed across the compound.

My eyes locked in on Axel's. *Oh, gods.*

Without a word, we took off at a sprint. The vault was home to some of our most treasured relics—nine of them, to be exact. If it was breached, and the crystals exposed . . .

My feet flew across the cobblestones. A burn erupted in my chest as I rounded the corner and drew a sharp breath. Janna and Torstein stood in front of the bungalow nearest the cliff. The black stream arched up before them. It swayed back and forth like a cobra ready to strike. Janna swiped valiantly at its base while Torstein sent ball after ball of fiery, blue sparks at its head. But the attacks were futile. The black tube slammed into them, driving them onto their backs and pushing its way through the bungalow's wooden door.

The vault was in there. If that monster got inside it . . .

I raced forward, reaching the entrance in ten swift strides. While I ran, I trained my eyes on the door. The smoke swept inside, coiling around the obelisk that guarded the entrance to the vault. It molded itself into a mist and pelted the pillar before sinking slowly to the ground.

*Did it actually get in there?*

I pulled Janna to her feet and called over my shoulder to Torstein. "We're in trouble."

"Did it—"

"The intruder went down the shaft," I confirmed.

Then I turned to our light mage. "I thought it was coded so it only opened for you. Well, for you *and* me, but that's—"

"It is." Torstein activated the light in his palms. He tossed a sharp, blue shard between his hands as he stepped into the bungalow. "This could be a trap. But if it's not . . . and if that thing has gotten to the crystals . . ."

"How do we get there first?" Axel asked.

"Ingrid," Torstein said. "Activate the entry."

"You're sure?" I asked.

"Do it."

With a nod, I transferred my sword to my shield hand. Then I lifted my palm to the obelisk, gritted my teeth, and waited for the pain.

It was prompt, swift, and unrelenting.

"Oh my gods." I cried out as the burn seeped into my palm. My hand melded into the rune of Tyr, our war god. It pulled me closer even as I instinctively pulled back. The stone's surface softened, and as quickly as it had come, the pain was gone. It had only been illusory—a protection Torstein had created to ward off intruders. But the sensation hadn't seemed to slow the smoke-snake. And if that thing was down there . . .

The stone released its hold on my hand. I quickly stepped backward as the obelisk lowered itself to the ground, revealing a small, round opening in the floor. It was barely wide enough to fit our shields, and I toyed with the idea of leaving mine behind. But as my brain flashed on the memory of my near death-by-impaling, I quickly rejected that plan. We'd need every tool at our disposal if we were going to stay alive down there . . . and we had to stay alive to stop our mysterious assailant from destroying everything we'd worked to protect.

"I'm going in," I announced.

"I'm right behind you." Axel followed me down the narrow, winding staircase that led to the basement vault. When we reached the lower level, we paused to assess our surroundings.

"Stone hallway lit by wall candles," Axel said softly. "No foreign presences detected."

"Janna and Torstein descending the staircase." I glanced over my shoulder. "No offshoot rooms, except the vault straight ahead."

"That must be where the assailant is," Axel said.

We crept slowly forward. We'd only made it five steps before Axel raised a closed fist. "Wait."

"What is it?" I paused mid-step.

"Wind. Do you feel it?"

I lifted my chin and peered over my shoulder. Sure enough, a light breeze swept down the staircase. It brushed against my cheeks, lifting my hair as it swirled around me in an invisible spiral.

"Get down, Shieldmaiden!" Axel threw himself into me. He pivoted as he fell, rotating so his body shielded mine from the impact. His back cracked against the stone floor a split second before I landed on his chest with a dull *thud*. Immediately, Axel rolled on top of me.

He covered my body with his as a biting wind swept along the hallway. The icy breeze pushed past my bare arms and sent a wave of goose bumps rippling across my flesh.

"It's the stream!" Janna shouted.

Footsteps charged along the hallway. Axel pushed himself off of me, then offered his hand to help me up. I jumped to my feet. We stood side by side, swords drawn, and ready to fight. The stream hit Janna and Torstein, slamming each of them into the wall. It swirled spastically in its quest to reach the vault's wooden door.

*It's so strong . . .*

"I've got it." Axel lowered his head and lifted his sword. He looked ready to charge.

But as quickly as it had come, the stream turned back around. It blew through the hallway, pushing me into Axel. Then it swept up the stairs and out of the bungalow.

What. The. Actual. Helheim?

"Check on the crystals," I shouted.

Torstein jumped up. He rushed to the wooden door and carefully unlocked it. When he pushed it open, a surge of blue light illuminated the corridor.

"One, two, three . . . they're all there." Torstein clicked the door closed behind him. "It didn't take anything. Didn't even try to breach this door. Why would . . ."

Janna leaned back against the stone wall. "What was that thing?"

"And why did it come this far only to turn around?" Axel stepped closer to me. He scanned my body before letting his gaze settle on my face. "You okay?"

"Never better," I said easily. "You?"

"A little bruised but fine." Axel jutted his chin at Torstein and Janna. "You two?"

"We're okay," Janna confirmed. "Just . . . confused."

"I don't understand." Torstein locked the door to the vault. "Why did it leave? And what *was* it?"

"And how did it breach the compound's barriers?" I asked. "I thought this was the safest place in Los Angeles."

Torstein ran one hand through his hair. "It was. It *is*," he corrected. "But until we know more, I'll double down on my protections. And reset the locks on this place."

He walked unsteadily along the hallway.

"I thought the stream had breached the obelisk," I said. "But it didn't come down until after we did. Right?"

"I honestly don't know." Torstein's normally smooth hair stood in wild disarray, and his serene demeanor had been replaced by trembling hands. "For the first time in a long time, I have no idea what's happening."

Janna and I exchanged worried looks. If our calm, collected light mage was shaken, we were *really* in trouble.

Whatever was happening, we needed to get to the bottom of it.

*Fast.*

## CHAPTER 5

O N MONDAY EVENING, IT was business as usual at Kappa Mu. It was time for our weekly Monday night dinner—a tradition in which each sorority and fraternity gathered for a family-style meal while roaming groups of pledges, club representatives, and members of the student government went from house to house to make their announcements. Sometimes it was frustrating to have a meal interrupted by a chorus of singing frat boys. And, of course, more efficient methods of communication existed. But the custom had worked its way into my heart. I was going to miss it when we left Los Angeles . . . *if* we left Los Angeles.

*Stop it, Ingrid. The mission is well under control.*

Sure, it was. *Snort.*

The night started out like any other. Janna, Brigga and I slipped into our little black dresses and walked down the winding staircase that led to the first-floor foyer.

"Whoa," Brigga whispered as she rounded the bend. "That thing is *huge.*"

I took another step and spotted the behemoth. *Yikes.*

"It's nearly as big as the tree in the castle," I whispered back. I peered over the railing to study the enormous Christmas tree standing proudly in the entry. Our housemates had spent most of the weekend decking the halls—filling every corner of Kappa Mu with trees big and small, multiple menorahs, and a bounty of boughs of holly. The main display—the one that would greet visitors as they walked through the door, and that was currently filling my nostrils with pine and cranberries—included a fourteen-foot, pink-and-gold-ribboned tree framed by two draped tables. The first was swathed in shimmering, blue and silver tablecloths, and covered in elegant, candle-laden menorahs. The second held a cornucopia of fruits and nuts, which circled a display of green, red and black candles. Strings of paper snowflakes stretched across the walls along with rows of fairy lights, which illuminated the space in a warm glow.

"They take their holidays very seriously here," Janna said.

I smoothed the skirt of my dress as I cleared the staircase and entered the wreath-covered dining room. "I'll say."

"Hey, Norway!" Meri stood behind one of the big,

round tables near the front of the room. Kayla, Devyn, and Ali looked up with warm smiles. "Come sit with us. We're planning a holiday dinner to celebrate all of the cultures within Kappa Mu, and we'd love to hear about the winter traditions you have back home."

*Oh gods!* I arched my brow at Janna as we claimed empty seats at the officers' table. Which traditions had survived the past one thousand years?

"Well . . ." I spread my napkin across my lap. "We, uh, we celebrate lots of thing."

It was true. From Odin to nature to Jesus, Valkyrians worshipped pretty much across the board. And between Solstice and Christmas, winter was prime celebrating season.

"But what's your *favorite* tradition?" Kayla passed me a plate of chicken. "Like for us, the village my mom was born in has a huge snow festival every winter. So we always go up to our cabin in Big Bear and do a snow blessing. And we call the hot tub our *onsen* because, well, why not?"

"And my family celebrates Hanukkah with all my aunts and uncles in Santa Barbara," Devyn offered. "We have a latke competition—best recipe wins bragging rights for the entire year. I am going to *crush* my cousin this time around. Ali gave me a tip about—well, I can't tell you what I'm putting into my latkes. You might tell Rachel."

"For the hundredth time, we do not *know* your cousin." Meri shook her head. "My family makes Norsk waffles and lefse, obviously."

"Obviously," I agreed. Gods, I missed Norwegian flatbread.

"And lussekatt buns for Saint Lucia—Saint Lucy's Day," Meri continued.

"You celebrate that now? Er, uh, here?" Brigga asked.

"Of course. It's one of my favorite traditions." Meri forked a potato, and brought it to her mouth.

"Mine too!" Brigga's eyes lit up. "It's a huge honor to be chosen to play Lucy. I got to do it when I was twelve."

"So did I!" Meri finished chewing. "Our school always did a big procession, since so many of the families in our town—state, really—are Scandinavian. And when we were finished, we'd go to the retirement home next to our campus, and the residents would sing 'Sankta Lucia' to us. It was fun."

"What's Saint Lucy Day?" Ali asked.

"It's a holiday that blends elements of the Winter Solstice with Christianity," Brigga explained. "It marks the importance of bringing light into a dark world, and involves candles, songs, and lots of good food."

"That sounds really nice," Kayla said. "What was Lucy the saint of?"

"Of light," Brigga said. "She was a young girl who brought food to people who were homebound. She wore a wreath of candles on her head, which kept her hands free to carry more supplies."

"She was taken prisoner, and her captors tried to burn her," Janna added. "But she was so good, and so full of light, the fire refused to touch her. Ultimately, she was stabbed."

"That's awful." Kayla winced.

"Yeah, well, she'd dedicated herself to God—which, of course, upset the guy who wanted to marry her." Meri shook her head. "Men just do not understand when a woman has *other* priorities. My father would much rather I just get married than go to medical school. But who says I can't do both?"

"You're going to be a healer?" I asked.

"A surgeon," Meri said proudly. "I just got into the program here at So Cal State. Since I'll be a local alumna, maybe I can be our interim house mother if Gertrude ever takes a vacation."

"Good luck." Devyn snorted. "Gertrude *never* travels."

I turned to Devyn. "What about you? You graduate in the spring too, right?"

"Yup." Devyn put down her water glass. "I've been interning with a publicist for the past two years. They're going to hire me as a junior team member in June."

"It's a *huge* deal," Ali enthused. "Devyn's company handles the top celebrities in Hollywood. Actors, musicians, that one really big politician who's *also* directing a movie . . ."

"I'm excited." Devyn's cheeks pinked. "And Ali's going to get her MBA. When do you hear back from that big fancy school back east?"

"Decisions go out in a few weeks." Ali held up her

crossed fingers. "If the Ivy League passes, there's always the West Coast. Though my parents will be crushed."

"You'll get into a great program, wherever it is," Kayla promised. "I believe in you."

"Aw, thanks K." Ali grinned. "And this time next year you'll be teaching kindergarten, and married, and—"

"I'm not even engaged," Kayla objected.

"You're *practically* engaged," Ali pointed out. "Promised to be pinned, which, in the Greek community, is engaged to be engaged. It's pretty much a done deal."

"Well . . ." Kayla blushed. "Yeah, I guess so."

"It sounds like women can do pretty much anything here." Janna put down her fork.

"Of course." Kayla tilted her head. "Are things different in Norway?"

Janna shot me a look. The truth was, things were different in *our* Norway. In most of the north, women were afforded very few rights. Viking-era women could own land and ask for divorces, but we were hardly going out and influencing politics or working as healers. Those of us lucky enough to live in Valkyris— where everyone was equal, and *anyone*, regardless of gender, could pursue the vocation of their choosing— worked to introduce our lifestyle to the rest of the territories. But minds were slow to change, and we'd made little headway during my brief tenure as a shield-maiden. It was good to know that things would eventually shift for the better—even if it was a thousand years in the future.

*I wonder what happens between my now and theirs?*

"Things are a little different in Norway," Janna answered Kayla's question. "But, you know, every region is unique."

"What Janna means is that the smaller towns are less progressive," Brigga said smoothly. I exhaled. Of course our disseminator had read up on contemporary norms. "But in the bigger cities, *naturally,* women pursue a variety of careers."

"Everyone should get to follow their passion," Kayla said earnestly.

"Agreed," Janna said.

As shieldmaidens, we literally fought for that right every single day.

"Ooh, the last group is here!" Kayla dabbed the corners of her mouth with her napkin. She turned her attention to the girls who'd lined up at the front of the dining room. They wore various patterns of red and green, and they stood with their hands clasped in front of their waists. Kayla rang the bell beside her plate, and with a cheerful, "Quiet, everyone!" she brought the room to silence. "Go ahead, ladies."

The brunette at the end of the row cleared her throat. "We're pledges from Gamma Alpha Psi, and we're here to invite you to our Christmas Cookie Bakeoff and Bake Sale."

The girls burst into a cheerful song, the lyrics of which outlined their favorite types of cookies, the prizes up for grabs, and the virtues of the charity their event would benefit—the Los Angeles Battered Women's Shelter. When they'd finished, Kayla promised full Kappa Mu support. Then we filed out of the dining room to freshen up before our chapter meeting. My heart tugged as I watched my "sisters" make their way up the stairs to their rooms. Each woman was fully invested in doing what she could to make her world a better place. They'd joined Kappa Mu not only to build friendships, but to improve their community and support one another as they made their way through life. The house I currently lived in was a squadron all of its own—one of modern-day shieldmaidens, whose honor and sensibilities continued the mission my teammates and I had set out to complete.

All we had to do was make sure Sverrir didn't destroy everything we'd *all* worked so hard to build.

Fifteen minutes later, Janna, Brigga, and I lined up downstairs with the rest of our sisters. When it was our turn, we stepped forward so Lexi and Becky could check us into the chapter meeting.

"I see you wore your pins this week." Lexi marked her clipboard.

"As we have every week since Meri loaned them to us." I fingered the tiny, gold triangle on my chest. Sorority pins were a pre-requisite to attending chapter

—a fact my friends and I had not known when we'd decided to pose as exchange students to protect our cover. Thanks to Meri's loan, we'd been spared the ire of the vindictive ethics chair. But the glare in Lexi's eyes made it clear that she was on the hunt for another victim. And, as always, I was Candidate Number *En*.

"Inga," Lexi said in her nasal voice.

"Ingrid," I corrected. Again.

"It's a shame you and your friends won't be joining us for the winter formal."

I crossed my arms. "What are you talking about?"

Lexi lifted a paper on her clipboard. "I never got your release forms," she said innocently. "They were due yesterday, so I can only presume that the three of you decided to sit this one out."

"We did not," Brigga objected. "I put them in your box last week!"

"It's a shame, really." Lexi twirled her pen. "I know Axel was really looking forward to going. Oh, well— maybe I'll let him escort me. That way he won't have to miss out."

A slow burn built in my chest. Lexi was the most insufferable, insipid, calculating shrew since . . . since . . .

"Don't worry." Brigga put her hand on my tensed bicep. "I've got this."

A thin smile tugged at my lips. Once upon a time, Brigga had been Valkyris' resident mean girl. I was only too happy to let her beat Lexi at what had until recently been *her* game.

"Lexi." Brigga pouted her glossy, pink lips. "Hard as this is to believe, I actually know what it's like when Axel isn't into you. It's awkward. And embarrassing. And it makes you want to wring the neck of the girl he actually *is* into."

Where exactly was she going with this?

"But the fact of the matter is, Axel *really* isn't into you. Not even a little bit. Not like he wasn't into me—because he was into me, for a little while at least."

Seriously. What was she doing?

"But that was before he met Ingrid," Brigga said, "who he is completely and totally into. So much so that he would never look twice at you. Not even if he was *absolutely* desperate, which of course, he'd never be. I mean, just think about him. Those muscles. That hair. That *gorgeous* face . . ."

"Brigga," I hissed.

"What? It's true." She shot me a wink before sidling up next to Lexi. "Now, think about how you will never, ever, *ever* have him. *Ever.* Because you are *totally* not his type. You're weak—I mean"—she pinched Lexi's frail-looking arm—"do you even bother to work out?"

"Excuse me?" Lexi's mouth fell open.

"You're not smart enough for him, either." Brigga shook her head. "Axel likes a girl who can challenge him. That's definitely not you."

"I'll have you know—"

"And you're ugly," Brigga finished.

I nearly choked on my laughter.

"What?!!" Lexi's nostrils flared.

"You're ugly," Brigga said matter-of-factly. "Not out here." She waved her hand around Lexi's face. "But in *here*." She tapped Lexi's chest.

The ethics chair swatted her away. "Don't touch me."

"I don't want to," Brigga said coldly. "And neither does Axel. Or Raynor, for that matter. That's right. I've seen you make eyes at him, *Becky*." She glared at Lexi's second-in-command. "So, back. Off."

She pushed past Lexi and marched into the chapter room. I followed after her, bumping Lexi's bony shoulder with my arm as I moved.

"Excuse me, Meri!" Brigga waved down the social chair. "Lexi says there's no room for us at the winter formal, but we turned our forms in *well* before the deadline, and we have every intention of attending."

"Lexi?" Meri waved the still-steaming girl closer. "Is this true?"

"We're short on rooms." Lexi forced the glare from her face. "Protocol dictates the newest members give up theirs. So I guess they *could* come . . . but they'd have nowhere to sleep."

"What is it?" I put one hand on my hip. "Did we not turn in our forms, or are there no rooms? Because your story keeps changing."

Meri's lips turned down in a frown. "I thought we talked about this. Lexi, I want you to stay behind when we finish our officers' meeting tonight. Sounds like we need to revisit whether you're truly fit to hold your chair."

Lexi's face turned the shade of a fresh apple. If steam could have shot from her ears, no doubt she'd have gone full kettle. She waited until Meri turned around and walked to the front of the room before jabbing her finger into my chest. "You'd better watch yourself," she warned.

"On the contrary." I flicked her finger away. "Sounds like *you're* the one who got put on notice. Come on, Brigga. Janna."

I made my way down a row of seats and took a spot near the center of the room. As my housemates settled in around me, I shot a glance over my shoulder. Lexi's nose wrinkled in distaste, and she let out a frustrated growl.

"Well done, Brigga." I turned to the blonde. "You really got under her skin."

"Yeah, well, it's not hard." Brigga shrugged. "Girls like her need to feel like they have power—especially over men. Take that away, and what are they?"

"Really mean?" Janna offered.

"Exactly." Brigga crossed her long legs. She smoothed the hem of her dress where it stopped just above her knees. "Oh, and Ingrid—I meant what I said. You and Axel really are perfect for each other."

My cheeks heated. "Uh, thanks."

"He'd have gotten so bored with me." Brigga picked a piece of lint from her shoulder strap. "I can't kick his butt in the training room."

"Some days I can't either," I muttered. "But I try."

"Well, keep at it," Janna said. "Somebody has to keep

his ego in check."

*Truth.*

"Hey, girls." Kenzi slipped into the chair beside me. "Did I miss anything?"

"Only Brigga crushing Lexi's hyper-inflated sense of self," I said.

"Shoot." Kenzi shook her head. "I'd have loved to see that."

Janna leaned forward. "We'll fill you in after the meeting."

"Okay, ladies!" Kayla clapped her hands. She stood behind the long table at the front of the room, and rang the president's bell. "This meeting of the Delta Tau chapter of Kappa Mu will now come to order. The first point of business is housekeeping. Cara? What do we have this week?"

Our softly spoken house manager picked up her parchment. "Winter break is a few weeks away, which means we'll have lots of girls moving out—for three weeks, at least—and just a few of us staying behind. I've posted a timeline for exit and re-entry in the mail-room, so make sure you check on those dates. And if you *are* planning to stay through break and you *haven't* told me yet, please do so asap. We want to make sure our chef knows how many freezer meals to prep, since we gave her Christmas week off to be with her family."

"Thank you, Cara." Kayla looked at her agenda. "Anything else?"

"That's it for me." Cara sat back down.

"Good. On to philanthropy. Blair?" Kayla held out

her hand.

"Well." Blair stood up. "It's almost time for our Dodge Climate Change fundraiser. Thank you to Morgan and Bree for signing up to organize the dodge-ball tournament brackets. And big thanks to Chelsea for volunteering to stage the set. It's really cool of your dad to lend us his snow machine."

"We're spending Christmas in Switzerland, so he doesn't need it this year." A tall blonde spoke up from the front row.

"Nice." Blair turned to Kayla. "And my mom's going to bring us some props from the studio lot—her show's on hiatus, so we should be good to borrow them for a few days. We just have to be *really careful* not to break anything."

"Wonderful. Thank you, Blair." Kayla made a note on her parchment. "Okay, Kenzi? Secret Santa?"

What the Helheim was a Secret Santa?

Our yogi friend stood up. "It's that time of year! Which means that each of you will find the name of your Secret Santa recipient in a sealed envelope in your mailbox. Rules are the same as always—gifts are not to exceed ten dollars, and they must be deposited beneath the tree in the foyer no later than the Sunday before winter break. We'll open gifts at our final chapter meeting of the semester."

Kenzi sat, then stood again. "Oh. And if you're stuck on what to give your selected sister, come to me. I've got a pretty good list based on everyone's pledge forms."

"Thanks, sis." Kayla glanced down at her agenda. "Looks like we're on to socials! Meri, the winter formal is in less than two weeks. What do you have for us?"

"First of all, we need to go over the formalities for *next* Monday's event. A certain pinning ceremony." Meri waggled her eyebrows.

Kayla ducked behind a sheet of black hair. "Right."

"So, I know this isn't a surprise, like most of our pinnings are." Meri shook her finger at Kayla. "But Mike *had* to go and pre-pre-propose for his pre-proposal."

"He's romantic," Kayla objected.

"Don't brag," Ali teased.

"My point is, we're still going to pass the candle. And all sisters with steady boyfriends or girlfriends will still wear red dresses while the rest of us wear black. But this time, we all know who the lucky lady will be." Meri jotted down a note. "The Alphas will come at the end of Monday night dinner, so make sure you're dressed appropriately *before* you come down to the dining room. Everybody clear?"

A chorus of cheerful yesses filled the chapter room.

"I know you packed light for L.A., so don't worry if you didn't bring red dresses," Kenzi whispered. "There should be a few in the castoff closet. And Kayla and I have extras if those don't fit you."

"Thanks," I whispered back.

"As for the winter formal, the bus will leave here at ten a.m. on the morning of the thirteenth," Meri continued. "The event is in one of the ballrooms at the

Hotel Del Coronado, which is also where we'll all be staying. You should have plenty of time to explore the island before you prep for the event. We've got hair and makeup people booked to come to the hotel for those who want to sign up, and I have a list of nearby salons if you'd prefer to go off-site."

Hotel Del Coronado. But wasn't that . . .

Janna reached over to tap my knee. "December thirteenth. San Diego." Her coffee-colored eyes were wide.

"Yes," I whispered. Oh gods. This wasn't good.

"The date and location of the planetary alignment," Brigga said quietly. "The dark mage's map said the energy would channel straight to San Diego."

"Which is also where the balboa bark is located. Which means . . ." My brain fought against the sheer number of coincidences.

Janna's fingers tightened around my knee. "Sverrir is going to be there on the thirteenth. In San Diego. At the alignment site."

"That's when he's going to enact his spell," Brigga whispered. "When he'll make his move to control the realms and wipe this world—and ours—right out of existence."

"That's when everything will come to a head." My eyes darted back and forth between my teammates. "We're about to have a front-row seat to the end of the world."

"No, we're not." Janna shook her head. "We're going to stop him."

Gods willing, my captain would be right.

## CHAPTER 6

**B**Y THE FOLLOWING MONDAY, my stomach was a massive ball of nerves. Not only had we failed to stop Sverrir, but we were no closer to doing so than we'd been the week before. Despite days of research, Brigga and Raynor had unearthed only a handful of balboa-related clues. They'd determined the plant was most likely a shrub, thanks to a series of oral histories in the rare books section of the philosophy library, of all places. The two-hundred-year-old text described our plant as "standing no taller than a young deer's haunches." It was something, at least . . . but we still had no pictures to go off. And despite his best magical efforts, Torstein hadn't managed to locate the plant.

We only hoped Sverrir was having the same problem we were.

"You're awfully quiet tonight, Ingrid." Morgan

nudged a platter of cobbler squares across the dinner table. "Aren't you excited about Kayla's pinning?"

"Hmm?" I looked up from the strap of my dress. Kenzi had loaned me the short, flared number, and its flaming-red fabric matched the ribbon around the Christmas wreath-candle holders in the dining room.

"You okay?" Morgan looked at me more closely. "I know sometimes pinnings bring up uh . . . feelings."

"Feelings?" I asked.

"You know." Morgan shrugged. "Seeing someone make a commitment can make a girl question the future of her own relationship, or re-evaluate whether her partner is someone she actually wants to be with for the long haul."

I blinked. I wanted to be with Axel for as long as the gods allowed it. No matter how much he irritated me, my heart was completely and totally his. It always would be. But our jobs were dangerous—there was no getting around that. We would *always* be fighting for Valkyris—for the virtues and beliefs our people held dear. But that meant that there would forever be a target on our backs. And we might not always be able to protect each other. I'd be there to cover Axel on the rare missions where we worked together. But when Axel was with the Airborne Assassins, or worse, when he was out in the field all by himself . . .

*What if I lose him someday?*

"Ingrid?" Morgan's hand on my shoulder pulled me out of my head.

"I'm good," I lied. "I've just got a lot on my mind."

75

"If it's school, I can help," Morgan offered. "We can study together for the folklore exam, or I can send you notes. Whatever you need."

"You're a good friend." I smiled. "We're really lucky to know you, Morgan."

"Thanks." Morgan's cherubic cheeks pinked. "Oh! Oh, listen! The Alphas are here!"

I pulled my attention off my dress and focused on the muted music coming from . . .

"Are they in the foyer?" Blair craned her neck.

"I think they're outside." Morgan clapped her hands together. "This is so exciting!"

Janna tilted her head. "I didn't take you for a romantic, Morgan."

"I'm not," Morgan said quickly.

Janna raised her palms. "You'll get no judgment from us. I know for a fact that Brigga has bought into this whole thing, one hundred percent."

She wasn't wrong. Brigga was literally on the edge of her seat, her cheeks flushed and her fingertips beating a frantic rhythm against her bare knees. Her glossy, blond curls bounced as she shimmied with excitement.

"Shh," Brigga hissed. "I don't want to miss a thing."

"Sisters of Kappa Mu." A hush swept over the dining room as Kenzi's normally serene voice cracked. "Tonight, we celebrate my sister taking the next step on her life's path. I've known Kayla literally my entire life. She's been my rock through fights with our parents, first crushes, and that time my jerk of a homecoming date stood me up—thanks for egging his car, sis."

Kayla's eyes crinkled at the corners. "He totally had it coming."

Kenzi smiled. "Kayla Takahashi has been a loyal member of Kappa Mu for every one of her years at So Cal State. She's embodied the epitome of our values—charity, service, and love. And tonight, she pledges her heart to the man who shares her drive to make this world a better place by serving their future community —he as a fireman, Kayla as an elementary school teacher. Are you ready?"

Kayla took her sister's hand and walked into the foyer. Nervous anticipation filled the air as the rest of us filed into the entryway and formed a big circle. One of the girls turned out the lights, leaving us all cloaked in darkness. Outside, the Alphas fell silent.

*Swish!*

The strike of a match brought a small flame to life. Kenzi clasped a glowing, white candle in her hands, then passed it to Ali. Ali shared it with Devyn, who gave it to Meri. The girls were silent as the candle slowly made its way around the circle. Morgan's hands trembled when it got to her, and my studious friend passed it slowly to Brigga, who reluctantly released it to me. When the candle reached Kayla, her red gown wavered around her trembling knees—her nerves must have gotten the better of her. She handed the candle to Kenzi, whose eyes sparkled with moisture as she passed the flame back. Kayla raised the candle to her lips, drew a shaky breath, and blew it out.

The strum of a guitar echoed from outside.

The front door cracked open, inviting moonlight into the foyer. Our circle parted as Kenzi led Kayla out to the porch. The rest of the girls pushed forward in a crush. Brigga wiggled her way right to the front.

*Of course.*

We all piled outside, a patchwork of red and black dresses, to find the Alphas on the lawn, each holding a long-stemmed rose. My eyes sought out Axel—his beard stood out in the sea of jacket-and-tie-wearing fraternity boys. But it was the twinkle in his eyes that held my attention. He followed the Alphas as they stepped forward, one by one, to present Kayla their rose. When it was Axel's turn, his nose twitched. As he stepped away, he swiped at it with the back of his hand. Was Axel Andersson *crying*?

"This is so beautiful." Brigga sniffled beside me.

My gods. My team was a mess.

When the last of the Alphas had given Kayla their flower, Mike offered Kayla his. He stared at her with complete adoration as one of his brothers moved to the front of the group and gave a humorous—and touching —speech. Apparently, Mike had been quite the partier until he'd met Kayla . . . and had now fallen head over heels in love.

"Kayla, I can promise you," the guy concluded, "that Mike is completely and totally devoted to giving you the best life he possibly can. You've made my boy a better man. And I am *honored* to present him for your consideration. Mike, go for it."

Mike dropped to one knee.

Every girl on the porch gasped.

Mike took Kayla's left hand. "It's no secret that I love you. You've owned my heart since the moment you skated into our Winter Wonderland exchange, twirled a circle around me, and picked my sorry butt up off the ice. You're the Leia to my Han, the marshmallow to my cocoa, the *only* person in this world who could not only put up with my bad jokes, but laugh at them."

"That's true!" Mike's friend called out.

Mike didn't take his eyes off our president. "And it would be my absolute honor if you would wear my pin."

Kayla nodded, tears streaming from the corners of her eyes. She leaned forward to cup Mike's cheek with one hand while he removed his pin from his jacket and stood.

"May I?" he asked.

Kayla smiled shyly. She swept her hair over her right shoulder and placed her white-tipped fingernails atop her chest. "I'll wear it proudly over my heart."

Mike fastened the pin, then swept Kayla in his arms. My eyes sought out Axel's, and I couldn't help but grin at the slow burn emitting from his eyes. The assassin was *clearly* into this whole over-the-top spectacle.

It was kind of cute, really.

I tore my eyes away from Axel and took in the scene

on the porch. Most of the girls were crying. Some dabbed delicately at their eyes with handkerchiefs they'd concealed gods only knew where. Others flat out sobbed, throwing their arms around one another in unabashed displays of emotion. On the lawn, the guys fared better—only Mike's best friend betrayed a hint of sentiment, while several of the Alphas hollered at the happy couple to get a room already. Janna nudged me with her elbow, and I followed her gaze to find Brigga at the front of the crying girl group. Our friend stared adamantly at Raynor, jutting her chin at Kayla and Mike, then back down to her own chest.

"I think she's telling him she wants to be pinned," Janna whispered.

"Pinning's not a thing in Valkyris," I whispered back.

"I have a feeling it's about to be."

*Oh, please. No.*

"I wonder how much we'll actually bring back with us," I said as the party flowed onto the lawn.

"I'm not sure." Janna followed the Alphas across our grass and onto theirs. The processional wound through a wooden gate, and when we stepped into the backyard the space was illuminated with fairy lights. Strings of white bulbs stretched from the house to the fence, and chest-high tables rested at intervals around the lawn. Desserts covered a big table, and a server stood behind a bottle-lined table on the patio.

"Drinks, ladies?" Axel appeared at my side. He carried two liquid-filled flutes in one hand.

"Thank you." Janna took one of glasses.

"Oh, Axel! How thoughtful of you!" Lexi appeared from out of nowhere. She snatched up the second flute, and tossed it back. Her back arched as she lifted her arm, making it impossible to notice the absurdly low neckline of her dress. Or the unnatural way she pushed out her chest. *Obviously,* she was doing this to steal attention. Thank gods Axel wasn't dumb enough to fall for—

*Oh, come on!*

I stared at Axel's glazed expression, and gave a none-too-subtle, "Ahem."

Axel's eyes didn't leave Lexi's chest.

*Seriously?*

"Mmm. That tastes *so* good." Lexi's tongue snaked out to catch an errant drop of her drink. She swept it slowly around her pouty, pink lips, then shot Axel a coy smile. One corner of his mouth tugged up in his typical, easy grin.

My boyfriend was *clearly* not in his right mind.

Lexi placed her red-painted fingernails on Axel's arm. "You look *amazing* in that coat. What is it? Armani?"

"Uh . . ." Axel didn't pull away.

A slow rage sparked in my gut.

"You know," Lexi said sweetly, "I still haven't chosen my date to the formal. I've had *so many* offers, but I'm still hoping . . ."

Her crimson talons crept over to Axel's chest. She rested her palm across his heart and sighed dreamily.

So help me gods, I was going to kill them both.

"Really, Lexi? You know he's with Ingrid." Janna crossed her arms.

"Oh, Inga. I didn't see you there." Lexi's eyes widened in mock-surprise.

"It's still In-*grid*," I growled.

"Po-tay-toe, poh-tah-toe." Lexi shrugged. She turned her attention back to Axel. "So? What do you say?"

"Uh . . ." My idiot boyfriend watched as Lexi adjusted the narrow strap on her shoulder. By accident or design—I was betting the latter—the movement plunged her neckline a half of an inch lower.

"What *do* you say, Axel?" Janna prompted.

Axel's head snapped up. Awareness swept through his grass-green eyes as he took in Janna's furrowed brow and my death glare. If looks could kill, he'd have been dead, wrapped, and set to sea in a Viking funeral of absolutely *blazing* glory.

*The jerk.*

I turned on one heel and stormed across the lawn.

"Ingrid. Wait." Axel was right behind me. Apparently, he'd snapped himself out of his Lexi trance.

*Whatever. They can have each other.*

"Ingrid!" His hand wrapped around my bicep. I whirled around and crossed my arms.

"What?"

"Hey." Confusion colored his perfect, traitorous face. *Jerk.* "I'm sorry?"

"For what, exactly?" I spat.

"I don't know," he admitted. "But you're obviously mad at me."

The rage in my gut surged in an inferno. "Seriously?"

He reached out for my arm. I stepped quickly backward. "If you're so into Lexi, why don't you just go be with her?"

Axel's brow formed a deep *V*. "Why would I want to be with Lexi?"

"I have no idea. But you obviously have a thing for her."

"And you obviously hate her." Axel shrugged. "I don't get it. Lexi's not that bad."

My hands balled into fists. I had to remind myself we weren't alone, and publicly screaming at one's idiot boyfriend was not something that was done in *any* era —no matter how much said boyfriend deserved it.

"Fine," I gritted out. "If she's not that bad, I'm sure the two of you can be very happy together."

Axel shook his head. "Jealousy's not a good look on you, Shieldmaiden."

*What the actual Helheim?* Did he *seriously* call me out? When he was *just* ogling another girl?

Axel reached over again. I took another step back. He exhaled in frustration. "Come on, Ingrid. You know you're the only one for me."

"Do I?" I crossed my arms. "Honestly, Axel. Sometimes I'm not sure where I stand with you."

Axel's jaw twitched beneath his beard. "How can you say that?"

"Everyone told me you weren't a relationship kind of guy." I forced my voice to hold steady. "I thought maybe you just hadn't found the right girl yet—that maybe things would be different with me. Which, I guess, is what every dumb girl thinks always."

"Ingrid." Axel's eyes turned down at the corners.

"Look, I get it. We're stuck on the same mission, so I was the obvious choice—a few weeks ago."

"What are you even—"

"But now that it looks like we're going to be here a while," I continued, "you want to keep your options open. It's certainly not what I wanted, but it is what it is. So, good luck to you—Lexi's a real backstabber, by the way. But you'll figure that out eventually. You and I can return to being work associates and pretend that none of this ever—oh!"

Axel stopped my speech with his lips. His fingers wove through my hair, holding me in place as he pressed his mouth hard against mine. I didn't push away. But I didn't relax into the kiss, either. For the first time in a while, I honestly didn't know where we stood.

Would Axel have actually chosen me if we *weren't* forced to be together on this crazy mission?

When Axel pulled away, his eyes blazed—with passion or anger, I couldn't quite tell. He placed his hands on my shoulders, held me at arm's length, and looked me straight in the eye. When he spoke, his voice came out in a soft growl. "You listen to me, Ingrid Tirsdatter. I do not now, nor have I ever, wanted to be with Lexi."

"Then why don't you tell her to back off?" *And why do you keep looking at her like that?*

Axel shrugged. "Because she's no threat to us. I know where you and I stand."

My toe nudged the grass. "I don't," I muttered.

Axel lifted my chin with two fingers. "Seriously? After everything we've been through?"

I averted my gaze. "I . . ."

"I'm not into Lexi," Axel said gently. "The only girl I'm into is *you.*"

My anger softened. "I'm into you too."

"I sure as Helheim hope so." Axel stroked my cheek with his thumb. "Now, are you done being mad at me? Or do I have to go eat those brownies all by myself?" He jerked his head toward the dessert table.

My mouth watered. "They have brownies?"

Axel slid his arm around my shoulders and guided me to the desserts. He heaped two brownies on a plate, and handed me a fork. "Chocolate's still your weakness, right? I mean, besides me?"

"Don't flatter yourself, Andersson. I like chocolate *way* more than I like you."

"And still, I'm not threatened." He shot me an easy grin. I dug into my dessert.

*My gods. This brownie.*

"Mmm. This." I moaned through a mouthful of sugar. "This brownie, this one right here. I have to

85

figure out how to bring *this* back with us. Valkyris is great, but it is sorely lacking in brownies."

"I'm sure you'll explain it in great detail to the chefs." Axel nudged his own utensil into the dough. "They're pretty good at replicating things, so you should be able to—hey!"

"Back off." I swatted my fork against his. "This one's all mine."

"But I got two," he objected.

I mashed them together and shielded them with my fork. "Leave it, Andersson."

Axel's eyes shifted over my shoulder. "What do you suppose is going on there?"

I followed his gaze to a table near the pool where Brigga waved her hands enthusiastically. Poor Raynor stood in front of her, looking for all the world like a cornered animal. His eyes were wide, his palms flipped upward, and he opened and closed his mouth as if he were unable get a word in edgewise.

"Any idea what that's about?" Axel moved on to the pie. He plated a slice, took a big bite, and mumbled, "S'good."

"I think Brigga wants some kind of commitment. Which is wild, because I swear it was just last week she was flirting with Torstein. So . . . my *gods*, this brownie is incredible."

Axel laughed. "That's Brigga for you. But Raynor's crazy about her. I'm sure he'll do whatever she asks him to."

I licked a crumb from the corner of my lips. *No brownie left behind.*

"What about you?" I teased. "Would you sing silly songs and declare your fealty to me in front of the entire Airborne Assassin team?"

"I would if you wanted me to." Axel lowered his fork.

Heat flooded my neck. "I was kidding."

"Well, I'm not." Axel studied me seriously. "I told you, you mean a great deal to me. More than all the dragons under my care."

My lips tugged up. That was high praise—Axel's dragons meant everything to him. "Even little Rufus? How's he doing, anyway?"

"He's fine. Don't change the subject. I know you're not into big declarations, so I won't force you to hear one. But there's very little I wouldn't do for you. Including singing in front of my squadron."

"*Ja*, well, I'm never asking you to sing. Or do . . ." I waved my hand around the yard. ". . . any and all of this."

Axel nudged me with his elbow. "Aw, come on, Shieldmaiden. Isn't there *some* part of you that finds it just a little bit romantic?"

"I mean . . . I guess." I forked another mouthful of brownie. "But public scenes aren't really my thing. I'd much rather a man save me from a fire monster. Or, I don't know, *row the boat home himself* after claiming to rescue me from a vitriolic Viking clan . . ."

"You're never going to let that go, are you? I was injured. We've been over this."

I set my utensil across the plate. "I'm just saying. You owe me a boat ride. That's all."

"Mmm." Axel stepped closer. "Maybe I do."

I tilted my chin back, and ran my fingers along his jaw. "You have pie in your beard."

"You have chocolate on your lips."

I slipped my arms around his waist. "What are you going to do about it?"

Axel placed his hand against the small of my back. He pressed my torso into his and lowered his head until his mouth met mine. His tongue swept lightly across my lower lip, and a surge of heat coursed straight through me. I reached up and wrapped my fingers through the silky strands of his hair. I loved it when he wore it down. The brown waves fell around his shoulders, framing his beard and making his eyes—

"Oh!" I gasped as Axel hiked me against his hip. The heat drove lower, sending shockwaves through my entire body. My chest melted against his, so my weight was supported almost entirely by Axel's strong arms. He deepened the kiss, and I tightened my grip on his hair. The entire world faded away until the only thing I knew was Axel kissing me beneath the fairy lights. I could have stayed lost in that moment forever.

But a delicate "ahem" forced Axel's lips from mine. His cheeks were flushed as he pulled back with an exasperated look.

"Yes, Janna?" Axel spoke through gritted teeth.

"I don't mean to interrupt. You do seem *very* busy."

"We *are* busy." Axel grunted. "So, if you don't mind—"

"I don't mind." Janna picked an invisible piece of lint from the bodice of her dress. "But Torstein might. He's right over there."

I followed Janna's pointed finger to the corner of the yard. Sure enough, the light mage stood with Raynor and Brigga. He raked his hands through his white-blond hair—an uncharacteristic nervous tic. Brigga's animated gestures had given way to a fervent wringing of her hands. Even Raynor's face appeared paler and more hollowed than usual. Something was definitely up.

Axel's lips would have to wait.

I reluctantly extracted myself from his arms. "Raincheck?"

"Count on it." He laced his fingers through mine, and led me across the sea of beverage-wielding revelers. When we reached our teammates, he leveled Torstein with a look. "Okay, light mage. Let's have it."

"I need you all to come with me," Torstein said solemnly. "Now."

"We're hardly dressed for work," Janna pointed out. "Should we change, or—"

"Do what you need. But do it fast." Torstein turned on one heel. He marched through the party, passing mead-carrying Alphas and a sea of excited K-Mus. A dark cloud seemed to hover around him as he stormed across the lawn.

My teammates and I hurried after him.

I glanced worriedly at Axel as I moved. As always, Freia's dagger was strapped to my body—tonight, I'd secured it against my upper thigh. But beyond that, I was weaponless. "Should we get our swords, or—"

"Yes." Torstein whirled around and lowered his voice. "Weapon up and meet me at the SUV. There's no time to lose. The crystals are gone."

Ice raced through my veins. "What did you say?"

"The crystals are gone," Torstein repeated quietly. "And if we want *any* chance of getting them back, we need to go. Now."

Axel's grip tightened around my hand. Our eyes locked in silent communication. We had to recover the crystals. We had to do it fast.

And we absolutely, without a doubt, *could not fail.*

## CHAPTER 7

TWENTY MINUTES LATER, WE arrived at the meditation center. Our drive had been mostly silent. Torstein had been absolutely fuming. He couldn't believe someone had broken into his compound—again. And he couldn't find the words to explain what had happened. He said it would be easier if he just showed us the surveillance footage.

Whatever was on it, it couldn't be good.

When the SUV pulled into Torstein's garage, I nudged Axel with my boot. His eyes met mine, and I leaned in to kiss his beard. The freshly trimmed fibers tickled my lips.

"What was that for?" he murmured.

"For luck," I said quietly. "I have a feeling we're going to need it."

Axel's lips turned down. "I have a feeling you're right."

Torstein slammed his door. Axel released his hold

on my hand, and we hurriedly stepped outside. The two of us unloaded weapons from the trunk while Janna, Brigga, and Raynor piled out of the SUV. In half a minute, we'd cleared the garage and were chasing after the white-blond blur of the light mage's streaming hair.

"Torstein," Janna called. "Wait."

"There's no time." He didn't break his stride.

Janna shot me a worried look as we wove our way through the bungalows. The moonlight cast a silent shadow on the cobblestone path. When we reached a building near Torstein's house, the mage threw open the door and waved us inside.

"In here," he said. "My assistant has us all set up."

"He has an assistant?" Brigga whispered as she slipped past me.

I followed her inside with a shrug. I'd never thought about how Torstein handled his business, but it made sense that he'd have help. Torstein ran a meditation kingdom. According to Kenzi, his spiritual center spanned three campuses, and included a veritable video empire. He probably had some serene-looking, über-earthy girl that fetched his green tea and essential oils while simultaneously coordinating his absurdly busy—

"Everything looks good, Magnus." Torstein nodded at a figure who looked to be more bear than man. He had a thick, bushy beard, a high, loose man-bun, and arms that were roughly the size of tree trunks.

"Will there be anything else, sir?" Magnus' voice

was far less terrifying than I'd expected. It was almost lyrical. And . . . soothing?

"That will be all." Torstein nodded. "You can retire for the night."

Magnus folded his hands together and bowed his head. Torstein copied the pose before crossing to the table at the far end of the conference room. A goblet of ice cubes stood beside pitchers full of colorful liquids. Beside them, a silver service set held what I assumed were coffee and tea—both emitted faint swirls of steam. White display stands hosted pastries and sandwiches, while matching bowls held dried fruits and an array of nuts. Had Magnus prepared all of this in the time it had taken Torstein to pick us up?

*Guru life must be good.*

"Help yourself to food. Drinks. Caffeine. Wheatgrass. Gods know I need some." Torstein poured himself a tiny glass of green, swamp-like liquid. No doubt it was blended to optimize maximal health. *Blech.*

"What exactly happened here?" Raynor poured himself a cup of tea before taking a seat at the conference table.

I snagged a mug of coffee, then slid into place beside him. As I sat, I tucked one leg beneath the other. I was grateful we'd taken the extra minute to change out of our formal clothes. My workout pants were stretchy, and would allow me to kick some serious butt if whatever had gotten Torstein so riled up deigned to return.

"I think it's better if I show you." Torstein threw back another shot of the green sludge. Then he picked up a thin, black box, pointed it at the screen against the wall, and dropped into a chair with a heavy sigh. "Watch."

The screen flickered to life. It showed the surrounding bungalows illuminated by silvery moonlight.

"Is this happening now?" Axel glanced outside.

"It's not a live feed, no." Torstein's eyes slid to the clock on the wall. "This was recorded a little over an hour ago."

I looked across the table to Torstein. "Can you explain this to us? We've never seen a . . . feed."

"I forget. You're not familiar with this technology." Torstein paused. "I have cameras set up all around the compound. It's for my security, of course. And to ensure the safety of the crystals in my care. Magnus reviews the footage at the end of each night and reports back to me with any anomalies."

My eyes widened. "Is he a mage too?"

"No," Torstein said. "Nor is he aware of my . . . proclivities. What he *is* is discreet. He worked as a bodyguard for several A-list celebrities before deciding he'd prefer a quieter, more spiritual path."

Janna stared at the screen. "Go on."

Torstein pushed a button on the black box. The images on the screen altered to show different angles of the bungalows.

"As you can see, we're looking at a completely ordinary evening in Malibu. Everything is calm, silent, and *absolutely normal*. Until . . ." He pushed the button again. This time, the images sped up. He waited for several seconds, before freezing the screen. "There it is."

My breath caught in my chest. *Oh, gods.*

"There what is?" Brigga asked.

"The smoke." Axel's jaw tensed. "It came back?"

"It came back." Torstein grimaced.

"I don't see anything." Raynor squinted.

Torstein stood and walked to the screen. "Do you see this faint, grey substance?" He pointed. "It's hovering about two feet above the ground."

"Now I do," Raynor said. "It looks like mist."

"It does," Torstein agreed. "Which may be why Magnus didn't alert me. At this stage, it appears to be fog creeping in from the ocean. Additional footage reveals that it came from the cliffs, which, to a casual observer, would make it even more fog-like. But to anyone who knows what went down last weekend . . ."

"It's the stream," I whispered. "It just changed forms."

"It adapted," Torstein confirmed. "The intruder knew we'd be looking for what we saw before—smoke. So this time, he sent in a stream of fog—one so thin, he thought we wouldn't notice. And unfortunately . . ."

"You didn't." Janna's knuckles were white. "So, what did it do?"

Torstein pressed a button. The screen resumed its slow scroll.

"The stream crept its way over the cliffs, along the

grass, and up the pathway until it reached the door to *this* bungalow." Torstein's lips set in a thin line.

"That's the vault," Axel said.

"It is. And you'll see what happens next."

My attention tunneled onto the image.

The stream snaked around the doorway, circling the frame three times before drawing back, as if in wait. It was so faint, it looked like nothing more than a light mist rising off the morning sea. But it suddenly coiled into a tight ball and struck the door like an attacking cobra, making it clear that this was no ordinary fog.

*What the Helheim is this thing?*

When the door refused to budge, the stream struck again. And again. *And again.* After a series of futile jabs, it pulled back. It stretched itself into a thin tube and slunk slowly toward the keyhole. It wormed its way inside, the movement jiggling the door handle as the fog gradually disappeared.

"I thought entry to that building required a retinal scan," I said. "Why is there a *keyhole*?"

"It's non-operational." Torstein sounded bewildered. "I decommissioned the mechanism. But obviously something as small as a mist . . ."

"What happened once it got inside?" Janna asked. "Do we have images of that, too?"

Torstein tapped the box, and the screen switched views. It showed the interior of the vault bungalow.

"The stream spends about a minute pushing its way through the keyhole. As I said, I altered the mechanism, so there can't have been much room." Torstein threw back another shot of green sludge. "Once it clears the door, it spends another minute forming itself into something palpable. Something capable of causing unimaginable damage."

"Oh, gods." I could barely hear Janna's voice over the pounding of my heart. If Torstein was saying what I thought he was . . .

Brigga gasped as the mist took on the outline of a human. A rounded gut and stringy hair formed from the wispy, grey smoke. The image grew denser until a jowly, cloak-clad man stood directly in front of the obelisk.

"Sverrir," Janna cursed.

For half a minute, the room was swathed in silence. Then every Valkyrian at the table erupted at once.

"What the actual—" Raynor pounded his fist on the table.

"He's inside the vault?" Brigga squeaked.

"How the Helheim did this happen?" Axel demanded.

"It shouldn't have," Torstein said. "I coded the compound to keep Sverrir out. I can only surmise that when he formed himself into that mist, he somehow eliminated his identifying properties. But once he's inside the entry . . . well, you'll see."

Dread coursed through me as my attention settled on the screen. Now fully formed, Sverrir raised his hand to the obelisk—to the rune of Tyr that I'd used to open it on the night of the last attack.

"He was watching us." My veins hardened to ice.

"He watched. And he learned," Torstein confirmed. "But at least *this* piece of protection couldn't be hacked. His energy didn't align with the key, which meant he couldn't open the entry."

"Then how did he get the crystals." Raynor looked from Torstein to the screen.

The guru's brows formed a deep *V*. "Despite being made of impenetrable stone, and despite being coded to grant entry *only* to those whose vibrations mirror my own . . ."

My stomach clenched as the man on the screen raised his fists and slammed them into the obelisk. A fierce *crack* rang from the screen as the column shattered. Its pieces crumbled onto the floor. Sverrir's boots crunched on the rubble as he took a step closer. He reached down, wrapped both hands around what was left of the structure, and wrenched it to the side. It was ripped from the ground, exposing the spiral stairway beneath.

Beside me, Axel swore loudly.

"I'm sure you know what happens next." Torstein increased the speed of the images. I held my breath as Sverrir quickly made his way down the staircase, entered the long, stone hallway, and blasted the door that guarded the crystals. The wooden surface splintered into shards. Sverrir quickly surrounded himself with a bubble so that the shards bounced off of him. They slammed into the stones of the wall before sliding to the ground. He marched undeterred into the vault, claimed the crystals for himself, and raised his hand. A swirling, black hole appeared in front of him. He stepped into it, carrying our entire stock of crystals . . . and any hope we'd had of saving our home.

Brigga leaned back her chair. "It's over."

"No, it's not. He still needs balboa bark. And Freia's dagger." I reached over my shoulder, my fingertips brushing against the blade strapped securely to my spine. "He'll have to kill me to get to it."

"Nobody's killing you," Axel vowed. "Or any of us. We just have to find Sverrir. And take our crystals back."

"How are we going to do that?" Raynor leaned on his elbows. "I'm assuming if he was traceable, Torstein would have done that already."

"You assume correctly." Torstein picked up another glass of the green goo—his fourth since we'd arrived. He swilled the contents around and crossed to the window, staring outside as he spoke. "I've been searching this region ever since the night he took the moonstone. Once I got that first read on him, I should have been able to trace him. But he's cloaked himself so well, it's almost as if he doesn't exist."

"Which leaves us with . . ." I looked at Axel.

"Not a lot of options," he admitted. "The alignment's in a week—that's when I think he'll try to enact his spell. He has almost everything he needs—give or take a few quanta crystals, but who knows if he needs a full set? Either way, he is *way* ahead of us in his world-destroying game."

"Great pep talk, Axel," Brigga said drily.

"I wasn't finished." Axel held up one hand. "As I said, our opponent *is* at an advantage. But we've come from behind before. On plenty of occasions. My team's been out-arrowed and outnumbered in countless battles. Our dragons have been shot down, mortally wounded, and in one case, turned against us *through no fault of our own.*"

I bit my tongue. This was no time to rehash his botched rescue attempt. But the memory of that horrible day—and the nightmare that followed—sparked a fresh wave of worries. Things went wrong for us. *A lot.* Dealing with magical beings and not-so-mythical creatures only increased the danger we faced almost constantly. I'd nearly lost Axel that day. And here we were again, fighting against an adversary whose abilities so vastly outpaced our own, that the likelihood of failure . . . of *death* . . .

A shudder wracked my spine. I couldn't go there. The thought of losing Axel was more than I was capable of processing. If anything were to happen to him, how could I ever forgive myself? *How could I possibly go on?*

"But in every one of those cases—*every single one*—we persevered." Axel spoke so earnestly, my heart swelled with admiration. "We triumphed over some extremely adverse situations because we had no other choice. And we're in that exact boat now. We're a few arrows short of a quiver—a *lot* of arrows, if I'm being honest. But giving up is not an option. Valkyris is unique in our era—we're the only clan in all of the north who believes in equality. In fairness. In doing the greatest good for the greatest number, and drawing out the skills of every worthy citizen, regardless of how they look or what they believe. We're unusual in our thinking, *but we shouldn't be*. If we continue to spread our message, to offer hope, then our way of life will one day become mainstream. But if we don't give this mission everything we have, there is a very real likelihood our world will be wiped from existence. Valkyris will be gone." Axel snapped his fingers. "And our way of life along with it. We may not know *how* we're going to come out of this, but we sure as Helheim have to try. So we're going to take five minutes to collect ourselves, have whatever pity party we need so we get it out of our systems, and then we reconvene and *figure this* dritt *out*. Everybody clear?"

My chest burned as worry gave rise to determination. "Crystal."

"Good. Now, get your butts outside and take a walk, or eat a sandwich, or chug more of that gross green stuff." Axel nodded at Torstein. "Do whatever it takes to get your life in order, and meet back here in five minutes. That's when the *real* work begins."

Janna banged her fist on the table. "Here, here."

"Ingrid." Axel pushed his chair back. "Come with me. Outside."

I snatched my sweater from the back of my chair and followed Axel. The brisk night air hit my bare shoulders and I threw my arms through the sweater's sleeves, tying the ribbon tight around my hips. It was cold—not Norway cold, but Los Angeles-in-winter cold. And the ice still thawing in my veins did little to warm me up.

Though the heat in Axel's stare wasn't going to hurt.

"Walk with me, Shieldmaiden." The assassin held out his hand.

I laced my fingers through his and let him lead us along the stone path. As we walked, knots tightened inside my stomach. Our chieftess had tasked us with preventing the fall of our clan, our culture, *our world.* And despite our best efforts, we were completely and totally failing her. And if we failed each other—if anything were to happen to Axel . . .

*Don't. Go. There.*

When we reached the end of the path, Axel squeezed my hand. "Coin for your thoughts." I blinked. Only a fifty-foot patch of grass stood between us and the edge of the cliff.

"You gave a solid pep talk back there," I said half-heartedly.

"But . . ."

"But . . ." I dug into the grass with the toe of my boot. "Things don't look good."

"No. They don't." Axel agreed. He tugged my body toward his, and slipped his arms around my waist. "We lost today's battle. But we haven't lost the war. Not yet."

I nestled my cheek against his chest, taking refuge from the wind. "Maybe. But we are *seriously* behind."

"We are," Axel said. "And truth is, I have no idea *how*

we're getting out of this one. It'll take a miracle for us to pull this off. But we have to play the long game."

"*Ja.* Well, let's hope the game lasts long enough for us to win."

"We'll win." Axel rested his chin on the top of my head. "We always do."

We stood in silence for a full minute. The whistle of the wind and the roar of the waves kept time with my thundering heart. I closed my eyes and breathed in Axel's comforting scent. We were a long way from home, facing insurmountable odds, and a seemingly undefeatable foe. But we had each other, and we had hope.

It would have to be enough.

Axel's thumbs drew lazy circles on the small of my back. "This weather reminds me of the day my dad taught me to sail."

I stilled. Axel rarely spoke of his parents. And he hadn't talked about them *at all* since we'd discovered they were still alive—albeit marooned on an island somewhere off the coast of Norway.

"Oh?" I said lightly, nestling closer to his chest.

"I was about seven years old, and Dad got me up early—when the sea was at its calmest. The sun hadn't yet come up, and this icy wind was whipping through Valkyris as we walked toward the docks. But, just like Dad promised, the eastern cove was protected. By the time we hit the water, the wind was gone." Axel chuckled, the deep sound resonating against my cheek. "I was so scared—I'd heard horror stories about boats capsiz-

103

ing, and in my mind, one wrong move could kill us both. But my father reminded me that we were in the calmest part of the water, and that we were both excellent swimmers. He had so much patience. I nearly tipped the boat half a dozen times before I managed to sail us up the length of the island." Axel's lips turned up. "He was a good teacher. And a wonderful father. I absolutely adored him."

I tilted my chin up to study him. Axel stared out at the ocean; his eyes locked on something far away. Axel's parents had been gone for most of his life. After their alleged death, Valkyris' chieftains had brought him into their family. And while he'd had a good life with the Halvarssons, it couldn't have been easy to suffer such an enormous loss at such a young age. But it wasn't Axel's style to dwell on what could have been. As he looked to the sea, his face hardened with resolve. No doubt he was working out a plan to capture Sverrir, to save Valkyris . . . to find a way home so he could track down his parents.

Gods, Axel was fierce. He'd faced so much in his lifetime—he'd fought to survive, he'd fought for Valkyris, he'd fought for me. But even when the odds had seemed impossible, he'd never lost sight of who he was, or of what truly mattered. He was the absolute epitome of strength.

It was time for me to be, too.

As terrified as I was to lose Axel—and half of my heart along with him—there was *no way* I could ever walk away. Being with him in the here and now was worth any amount of pain I might ultimately suffer. His strength, valor, and kindness were more than enough to get me through whatever horrors stood between us and our happily ever after. And if that future never came to pass, well . . .

At least I'd have lived my life with no regrets.

"I can't wait to meet your father," I said quietly.

Axel's gaze shifted to me. "Hmm?"

"I can't wait to meet him. When all of this is behind us. And your mom, too."

"*Ja.*" A wistful smile played at Axel's lips. "You're going to love them."

"If they're anything like you, I have no doubt." I stood on tiptoe and pressed my lips to his. When I pulled away, Axel tightened his hold on my back.

"We have a lot working against us, Shieldmaiden. But we have something huge to fight for." He lowered his forehead so it rested lightly against mine.

"Our future," he said at the same time as I said, "For Valkyris."

"Exactly." He kissed me again—deeper this time, so heat flooded my body. When my knees wobbled, Axel pulled me closer. A soft sigh escaped my lips as I curled up against him, forgetting everything but the warmth of his mouth on my neck and the light pressure of hips against mine. The only thing I wanted in this moment was—

"Ingrid. Axel." Janna's voice broke the spell. "Inside, now."

"Janna," Axel groaned. "I said to take five."

"*Ja.* Well, Torstein just got a hit. There's a crystal nearby."

Axel and I leapt apart.

"Where is it?" I dropped into a fighting stance.

"Is Sverrir on his way?" Axel spun a tight surveillance circle.

"Just get inside." Janna glanced at the clouds overhead. "We can't be too careful anymore."

Axel and I exchanged a look before jogging toward the conference room. If Torstein had read a crystal, it was likely that Sverrir had too. And if we could catch him in the hunt . . .

It was just the opening we needed. Now all we had to do was seize it.

By the time we reached the bungalow, Torstein had already summoned poor Magnus—who lived on the grounds and was used to being awoken at odd hours. The burly assistant quickly procured a set of climbing equipment. He worked with Janna and I to set up an intricate series of routes down the cliffs before returning to bed. When he'd gone, Axel, Brigga, Raynor, Torstein and I stood at the edge, while Janna barked instructions.

It was crystal hunting time.

## CHAPTER 8

"**B**E CAREFUL! THE CLIFFS** are slick, so make sure you're properly harnessed before you step off." Janna spoke from the edge of the seaside ledge.

"You're sure there's not an easier way down?" Brigga peered anxiously over the cliff.

"Not one that's this fast." Janna adjusted her shield on her back. "Torstein says the new stone is located directly below us—on a stretch of beach inaccessible by car, which means that even if we did drive down, we'd still have to hike in. It'll be easy. I promise."

"Says the shieldmaiden." Brigga shook her head. "You and Ingrid climb these things before breakfast. I'm a disseminator. I've never even—"

"I'll be right below you. I'll catch you if you slide." Raynor promised. "Besides, you're clipped in. Nothing bad can happen."

"Mm-hmm." Brigga didn't look convinced.

"Now, this equipment is a bit different from what

we have back home." Janna pointed to the metal ring attached to her harness. "These clips will hold us to the ropes. This device here"—she gestured to a metal mechanism—"will let us slide down slowly. Just crank it like so, and you'll manage your descent just fine."

She gave a quick demonstration.

"That seems pretty straightforward," Brigga said begrudgingly.

"It is. I promise." Janna put her hands on her hips. "I don't have to tell you all that time is of the essence. We all know Sverrir can port in and out via that mysterious black hole. And we all know he's likely to show up without warning. So get down as quickly as you can. Draw your weapons the moment you touch down. And *be safe.*"

I raised my fist. "For Valkyris."

"For Valkyris," the rest of our team echoed.

"Raynor and Torstein, you're up." Janna stepped away from the ledge. "Clear any tangles in the rope so the next parties have a smooth descent."

"Of course." The warrior and the mage each clipped in. They slid over the ledge.

"It's not bad," Raynor called after a moment. "But the wind's stronger than you'd think, so watch for swinging—oh, good gods! Get off of me!"

Janna dropped to her knees. She peered over the side. "You all right?"

"Torstein blew into me," Raynor muttered. "You know you could have ported yourself to the base of this thing, right?"

"I can't sustain my read on Sverrir when I go into a void," Torstein called back. "And I don't want to lose it in case—"

*Crack.*

"What's happening?" I released Axel's hand. We both ran to the ledge. I dropped to my knees and peered over. A fresh gust of wind whipped my hair across my face . . . and pushed Raynor directly into Torstein.

"Ow!" Raynor yelled.

Torstein rubbed his ribs. "You have bony elbows."

"*Ja*, well, you have a bony head." Raynor ran the hand not holding the rope over his shoulder. "There are no winners on this mountainside."

"Sverrir's going to be the big winner if the two of you don't stop talking and *hurry up*," Janna growled.

"Yes, ma'am." Raynor and Torstein continued their descent.

"Ingrid, since you're our strongest climber you're going to guide Brigga," Janna said.

I shot Axel a triumphant look. "Why yes, Janna. I *am* the strongest climber."

"Only because I taught you everything you know," Axel challenged.

"You didn't teach me to climb," I retorted. "Janna did."

Axel's lips flapped open and closed before settling into a puckered *O*. He looked like a fish caught out of water. "Huh. You're right."

"I usually am." I clipped myself in and wrapped my

hand around the southernmost rope. The wind was blowing from that direction, and it would be easier for me to avoid hitting Brigga than the other way around. "Okay, Brigga. You ready?"

Her face was determined. Her voice was anything but. "Ye-ees?"

I went with the face. "We descend on three. *En. To.*"

"*Tre.*" She took a tentative step over the ledge. "Oh, gods. It's windy."

"I know." I dug my toes into two tiny crevices and held tight to the rope. With a series of small steps, I crept down the side of the cliff, keeping a careful watch on my charge. The wind whipped my hair against my cheeks, and I tucked my face to my shoulder as I climbed further down. "Just dig your feet in and stay with me. Looks like there will be lots of toeholds in here, so you can always latch into the rocks if you—"

A fierce gust blasted the rocks. I turned my head to shelter my eyes.

"Hold on," I warned.

"Definitely am," Brigga gritted.

After an insufferable half a minute of gusts, the wind finally let up. "Okay. We can move again."

"You first," Brigga said.

I glanced down. Raynor and Torstein were nearly to the sand. They looked to be a good two hundred feet below us. This cliff was substantially higher than the ones back home. But even with the wind, the descent was much more manageable. Climbing equipment had come a long way in the past thousand years.

Brigga and I continued to make our way downward. My teammate did a great job—she wasn't particularly fast, but she listened to my instructions, and we inched carefully toward our destination. Everything was going well . . . until the wind changed directions.

"Ow!" Brigga's knee slammed into the rock.

"You okay?" I shoved my fingertips into breaks in the rocks and flattened myself against the stones. "Dig your fingers into a crevice—there are lots over here."

"I'll try." Brigga's voice wavered.

"And just hold tight." I pressed my cheek to the stone. "This gust should pass soon."

Brigga shrieked as she swung away from the rocky wall. A second later, she slammed into the hard surface, crying out as her shoulder made contact with the cliff. "Make it stop!"

"Push your fingertips into one of the holes!" I called.

"I'm trying!" Her arms flailed wildly.

*No!* She wasn't going to fall. I wouldn't let that happen.

"Forget it. I'll come and get you," I called.

I released my hold on the rope and wedged my fingers and toes into the cliff's tiny openings. There were enough small ledges that I'd be able to starfish my way to Brigga. I pulled myself closer to the wall and carefully placed one hand over the other until I'd made my way to Brigga. The wind hit me with a fresh blast, freezing my cheeks and icing my back. But I ignored the pain, directing my focus on Brigga's trembling hand.

I reached out one arm. "Hold on to me!"

"Okay!" she shouted back.

Her icy fingertips wrapped around my wrist. I pressed the heel of my hand to the rock, then reached around to push Brigga's fingers into a crevice.

"Hold here," I instructed. I released her hand and slung my arm around her waist. "I'll keep you steady until the wind dies down."

"Don't say *dies*," she yelled.

"You know what I mean."

I braced us both, holding tight until the worst of the gust had passed. Once we were all clear, I released Brigga. I dug the toes of my boots into a ledge and shouted my instructions.

"It's blowing at pretty fast intervals, so we're going to make our way down as quickly as we can. Forget the slow descent—we're going for a rapid rappel."

Brigga nodded. I couldn't be positive, but from this distance it looked like she was gritting her teeth.

Hard.

She didn't complain as we made our way down. I matched her pace, careful to keep a few feet below her so I could reach over to steady her rope . . . or, gods forbid, catch her if she fell. She only needed my help once—to navigate around a sizeable nest an enterprising bird had placed atop one ledge. When our feet hit the sand, Raynor ran over to help her unclip.

Brigga exhaled loudly. "Can we *never* do that again?"

"No promises." I released my hold on the rope. My legs wobbled as I removed my harness, reminding me why climbing workouts were a regular part of my routine back home. Ever vigilant, I swept my gaze in a swift circle and took inventory of my surroundings. The craggy cliffs gave way to a row of rubble, which in turn ebbed out to the stretch of yellow sand. Waves crashed against the coastline in rapid succession, the spray of water leaving foamy residue along the shore. The area in which I stood was roughly thirty feet deep by fifty feet wide, and was bordered by towering cliffs. Interspersed among the walls were bleak-looking caves and sharp-edged boulders. A rock-strewn tidepool sat along the north edge of the beach. By all accounts, it was a perfectly ordinary—albeit cold—stretch of coast. But I'd learned the hard way to never take chances. "Raynor, did you check the perimeter?"

"We're secure," he confirmed. "Torstein's scanning for the crystal, but . . ."

I eyed the light mage. He stood at the edge of the sea with his eyes closed and his hands raised. "Did he lose it?"

"I think so." Raynor frowned. "But he's not talking."

I glanced up. Axel and Janna made their descent. "Well, he's got another minute to find it. After that, we're searching the old-fashioned way."

"Agreed."

I drew my sword and pulled my shield from my back. Although Torstein had said this stretch of sand was inaccessible by car, it was still best to be on our guard.

Luck favored the prepared, after all.

I paced the small beach. At the edge of the sea, our light mage stood still as a statue. He turned in a circle, his palms moving slowly up and down as he did . . . whatever it was that he did while looking for magic rocks. After two rotations, he dropped his arms, opened his eyes, and walked back to us with a frown.

"Still no read?" Raynor called out.

"No," Torstein confirmed.

From ten feet above, Axel swore. "You mean you lost it?"

"I didn't lose it," Torstein said. "It's just . . . hiding."

"Explain." Janna touched down on the sand. She hurriedly unclipped and drew her weapons. Axel finished his descent and did the same.

"The signal is here. Occasionally." Torstein folded his hands together. "But it comes and it goes. It may have something to do with the sea. It's high tide, and it's always harder for me to track a submerged object."

"You found the last one underwater," I pointed out.

"True." Torstein paused. "Which means this one must have two blockers. Hmm. I wonder . . ."

He turned to the cliffs and held up his palms.

"You think it's inside the rock?" Axel shook his head. "We didn't bring axes. Or shovels."

"They use *drills*, now." Brigga offered. "Mechanized tools that turn in rapid rotation to—"

"Shh," Torstein said. "I have something."

Raynor looked at Axel. "We *are* cutting into the rock."

"We are not." Torstein lifted one finger. After a

114

moment, he turned it toward the northernmost boulders. "We're going around those. After the tide flows out."

"Huh?" I glanced at Janna. My captain just shrugged.

"The crystal is in a cave," Torstein explained. "One that's currently submerged, thanks to the tide. It will be accessible when the water pulls back."

"And when exactly will that be?" Janna asked. "You said yourself, we're kind of in a time crunch."

Torstein looked at the moon. "The water is ebbing now. If you don't mind wading in, we should be clear pretty soon."

"A little water never bothered us," Axel said.

"Good." Torstein walked toward the boulders.

I followed him, scanning the sea as I walked. "Let's get into position. If everything goes well, we can extract the target and have it back to the compound in—"

"What's that?" Brigga asked from behind me.

I turned around. "What's what?"

"That pulsing light." She pointed to the boulder.

Torstein pivoted with a grin. "That's our crystal. The water must be lower than I'd thought."

"Not low enough to get around that massive rock," Brigga pointed out.

"Who said we needed to go around it?" Axel ran forward, scaling the boulder like a mountain goat. When he reached the top, he turned to give me a triumphant grin. "Now who's the best climber?"

"Seriously?" I sheathed my sword and ran across the

sand. Locking my shield around my forearm, I raced up the side of the rock. "I am. Obviously."

"I beat you here," he challenged.

"I halved your time," I countered.

"You slipped on a mid-level toehold," Axel said. "Style points docked."

My eyes narrowed to slits. "Oh, bring it—"

"Do I need to separate you two?" Janna cleared the boulder. She dropped into a squat beside me. "You're distracting me from that."

I followed her point. Inside a waterlogged cave flashed a faint, blue light.

"It's definitely in there." Torstein spoke from Janna's other side.

"Now it's a waiting game." Raynor helped Brigga climb the rock.

We sat in silence for several minutes. Axel and I took turns scanning the beach for intruders. The only movement came from the waves, the sea-foam, and the occasional cawing bird. There wasn't a soul anywhere around.

*Unless they're staying hidden . . .*

I couldn't ignore the dread gnawing at my gut. On the surface, this leg of our mission was going well. But so many of them had started that way . . .

And so many had taken a horrible, horrible turn.

"The tide looks low enough." Torstein finally broke the quiet. "I'll go in first. I'm not reading any additional presences, but watch my back and be prepared to pull me out if . . ."

"We've got you." I climbed down the boulder and landed with a splash in two feet of freezing seawater. A chill swept up my legs, sending goose bumps rippling across my arms. The ocean in Malibu was considerably colder than it had been in Manhattan Beach. Maybe there was some kind of a current that reached this region.

*Or maybe it means trouble is coming.*

I kept my sword raised and my shield at the ready. If there was anything out of the ordinary, I was sure as Helheim going to face it fully armed.

We marched through the surf, wading toward a massive stone arch. Its surface was covered in barnacles and the shimmery, white remnants of saltwater, giving it a bumpy sheen that reminded me of the caverns near Valkyris. We walked for another minute before pausing outside the entrance of the cave. It was narrow enough that we had to enter single file, and so low that Axel and Raynor both had to duck to fit. Inside, it was dark—the passage was lit only by the faint glow of moonlight, with a secondary light source coming from somewhere to the south.

"There's another entrance down that way." Torstein pointed to the light. "Looks like it has a bigger mouth, so be on your guard."

"Noted." I shifted so my sword faced the unseen passage, then side-shuffled the rest of the way into the cave. After a short walk, the entry widened. I followed my team into a massive, waterlogged space.

"Holy Mother Frigga," Janna whispered. "This place is enormous."

"I've never seen a sea cave this size." I turned in a slow circle. "It must be as big as Valkyris Castle."

"Bigger." Axel came up beside me. "Is this normal for your region?"

"I'm not sure." Torstein opened his palms and shot twin fireballs at the cave's ceiling. They hung from the ceiling, two flaming chandeliers that illuminated the space and gave me a chance to study its interior.

Its *gargantuan* interior.

The cave was easily ten stories tall and fifty yards wide. The bottom half of its walls were the same shimmery-white as the outside arch, suggesting it was regularly filled with seawater. But the top half was a rich, buttery gold. Craggy rocks jutted from the walls, and pointed peaks stretched down from the ceiling—stalagmites or stalactites. I could never remember which was which. Torstein shot a series of flames at the walls. They clung to the rocks, creating a row of sconces that offered additional light. When he lit up the far corner, a second flashed pulsed. I squinted my eyes until I made out its source. Wedged into the absolute farthest crack of stone . . .

"There it is." I slogged toward the glowing, blue light. "The crystal is over there."

"Yes." Torstein moved along beside me. Each step sent an icy splash up my torso, but I ignored the chill and pressed forward. We were close—*so close*. The prize would be in my grasp in ten . . . nine . . . I counted slowly backward until I made it to the wall. Stretching out my hand, I wrapped my fingers around the crystal and raised it triumphantly above my head.

"Got it. Augh!" I cried out as a blast of cold shot into my hand. It burst through my skin and entered my body, sending rapid pulses of ice coursing through my veins. The pulses made their way up my arm and traveled across my shoulders before spiking into my head. Instant agony broke through my skull as ice picks jabbed angrily at the backs of my eyes. I wanted to drive my fingers into them—to claw the pain straight out of the sockets. But I brought my other hand to the crystal and held on tight.

I wasn't taking any chances.

"Ingrid!" Axel's shout echoed through the cavern. "What's happening?"

"I don't know!" I gritted my teeth and waited for the pain to pass. When it didn't, I stumbled toward the sound of Axel's voice. The cave blurred in and out of focus as I slogged my way through my discomfort. "The crystal is cold—*really cold.*"

"Give it to me." The assassin's deep voice resonated in my ear. "I'll hold onto it until—"

Air hissed through Axel's lips as he wrapped his hands around mine. The second I released the stone, relief coursed through me and my vision returned to normal. But the pain must have transferred to Axel, because his nostrils flared as he said quietly, "This is *way* more than cold."

"I know." I whirled on Torstein. "Can you stop it?"

"I don't think it's the crystal's doing." Torstein stood with his shoulders squared to the cave's entrance. My stomach clenched at the pinprick of darkness swirling just above the water. It slowly grew, the black circle shooting out snowy shards. Once it was large enough to frame three fully grown bears, it sent out an icy blast of wind. The gust struck hard, forcing me to dig in my heels so I didn't tumble over. Axel's teeth chattered violently behind me.

"It's. Trying. To. Escape!" His hands shook around the crystal.

"Just hold on," I called. I threw myself in front of him, using my body to shield both him and the crystal from the dark hole. All around me, my team readied for battle. Janna banged her shield, Brigga pulled her dagger, and Raynor gripped his sword in both hands. Torstein stood slightly in front of us; he'd be our first line of defense. The light mage turned his palms together and flexed his fingers. A white orb popped between his palms, its sinewy fibers emitting bursts of light that no doubt would have flattened even the most lethal Viking warrior.

But we weren't dealing with Vikings. And the only warriors in sight were standing at my side.

As I held my sword aloft and tried not to worry about the fact that my assassin boyfriend had been reduced to a trembling, shivering shell of his normally lethal self, we were joined by something far worse.

Frozen, white fingers with frosted, blue tips wrapped themselves around the edge of the portal. The fingers grew into arms, then an oversized, rail-thin body. Gangly legs stepped through the hole, splashing into the water with a steam-producing hiss. The blue and white anomaly turned its icicle-laden head. It scanned the cave until its black eyes zeroed in on me. Or, more likely, what was directly *behind* me. Blue flames sparked in its eyes as they locked in on the crystal.

The crystal currently being protected by the assassin who owned my heart. Oh, gods. If that monster went after Axel, my boyfriend wouldn't stand a chance. And if anything were to happen to him . . .

I raised my shield and dropped to a fighting stance. "You'll have to go through me first," I growled.

The frost monster snorted. White smoke flared from his nostrils as he lowered his head, crooked his razor-sharp fingers . . . and charged.

## CHAPTER 9

THE ATTACK WAS SWIFT. The frost monster cleared the room in seconds, his long legs making easy strides through the water. He was nearly to Torstein when the mage fired his white orb. The projectile struck the monster's chest, stalling him long enough for me to give Axel one instruction.

"Run."

The assassin didn't hesitate. He tucked the crystal beneath one arm, drew his broadsword with the other, and raced for the southern wall—the one closest to the large entrance to the cave. I raced after him, my speed slowed considerably by the two feet of water still filling the cavern. Loud splashes echoed through the space, and when I turned my head the monster had changed course. Instead of battling Torstein, his blue flaming eyes were fixated on Axel. He stomped across the cave, intent on pursuing the one person in all the world I most wanted to keep safe.

"Frosty's pretty determined," I yelled to Torstein. "Can you stop him?"

"I'm trying." Torstein threw a light beam at the creature. It grazed Frosty's shoulder, but the monster didn't stop. Torstein sent a second, then a third, each slamming into Frosty's back and shaking loose a layer of ice. The fourth beam struck Frosty in the head. This time, the beast paused long enough to shoot an irritated glare over his shoulder. He opened his mouth, turned his head to Torstein, and let out a battle cry.

"*Rrrroooooaaaarrrr!*"

Fist-sized ice balls barreled from Frosty's throat. They launched at Torstein, who promptly threw up a bubble of protection. The ice missiles bounced off the barrier, landing in the water with loud *plops*.

"Any chance the rest of us could get bubbles, too?" I shouted.

Torstein sent another series of beams at Frosty, then shook his hands and turned them on me and Axel. A single, filmy layer surrounded us both, stretching across the ten feet that separated us. When the protection sealed, he sent streams from each hand. One shot over my head, encasing Brigga and Raynor, while the other closed tightly around Janna. I ran harder, closing the distance until Axel and I were side by side. But the big entrance was still a way away, and Axel seemed to be struggling with his contraband. The crystal wrenched violently beneath his arm, pulsing brighter with each step he took.

"It's trying. To get. To. The. Portal." Each word came on a pant.

"Why would it do that?"

"No. Idea." Axel grunted.

"*Ja.* Well." Frosty let out another roar. This time, the ice balls bounced off of our shared bubble.

"Ingrid!" Brigga yelled. "Look out!"

A loud rip spiked my heart rate. From the corner of my eye, I noted Torstein's stream of beams, Raynor's swinging sword, and Brigga charging at the monster, her dagger raised overhead. But what was most concerning was the enormous white arm arcing above me. It drove what looked to be a three-foot icicle into my apparently not-so-impenetrable bubble.

"Torstein!" I screamed. "It's not working!"

"The ice spear must be laced with dark magic! Nothing else could have pierced this shield." Torstein fired off a fresh series of beams.

Frosty barely even flinched.

"What the Helheim?" Axel swore.

"That protection won't deflect dark magic. And I can't reverse its effects, so steer clear."

*Great.*

I pumped my legs harder. The exit still seemed miles away.

"The crystal's still fighting me." Axel's chest wrenched to the right. He lurched in front of me, and I slammed into his back.

"Uff!"

"Sorry!" Axel curled into a ball and I launched over

him. I rotated as I flew through the air, turning so I'd land on my back. The water broke my fall, the sharp sting of impact sending a shock wave across my skin. No doubt I'd be sporting an unwieldy bruise in the morning.

*Riiiiiiip!*

A flash of white sent me scrambling to my feet. Frosty's ice dagger had just ripped another hole in our bubble.

Axel and I had to get out of there.

"Head to the portal!" Axel shouted.

"What?" Had cold water and terror addled his brain?

"I can't. Fight the crystal." He spun in a tight circle. "And I don't want to hand this. *Ugh.* Over to him. We have to. Go to. The portal."

Behind us, Frosty's fingers jammed into the fresh tear.

"He's getting inside," I yelled.

"Then we go right on three. *En. To. Tre.* Move!"

We hung a sharp right. The monster kept moving forward. With one last rip, our protection tore fully open. We were exposed, outmanned, and, in all likelihood, running straight into a trap. But we'd been mere feet away from death-by-frost-monster. Maybe running headfirst into a dark passageway was the lesser of two evils.

*Oh, gods. What am I doing?*

"A little help here!" I shouted as I ran. Behind me, my team fought hard against our foe. Brigga leapt in the air and jammed her dagger into Frosty's thigh. The next second, Raynor swung his sword at the monster's knees. Ice chunks went flying as his victim raised a spindly arm to deliver a fierce backhand. Raynor flew across the water, bouncing like a skipping rock before slamming into the unforgiving cave wall. Janna picked him up. She gave a fierce battle cry before rushing back into the fight. And Torstein, well . . .

The light mage appeared to be staging some kind of aquatic attack. He held his arms in front of him and pulled them in a circle, as if he were stirring an enormous pot. The air around him spun. It shifted until it formed a vast whirlpool around the monster's feet.

"Ingrid!" Axel shouted. "I can't. Hold. On!"

I refocused and ran faster. Without breaking my stride, I sheathed my sword, then launched myself at Axel. I angled my shield, positioning it between the portal and the crystal. The stone flew from Axel's hands. It struck my shield with a force that shook my arm. But instead of flying into the dark abyss, it splashed into the water at our feet. Axel and I threw ourselves on top of it. We struggled to wrestle it into submission while the room exploded in chaos.

A deafening *boom* thundered. I lifted my head. Frosty flailed his ice-covered arms. His knees buckled and he dropped hard. He landed on his backside with a furious hiss.

"Got the crystal," Axel yelled.

I tore my attention from the enraged frost monster. Axel sat in two feet of water, his torso curled over the vibrating crystal. A bright blue emanated from his chest as the stone pulsed. It was almost as if it were calling out to . . .

"Oh. My. Gods." I stared at the *second* blue light. The one pulsing from inside the portal. "Do you see that?"

"See what?" Axel's chin was lodged against the struggling stone.

"Stay there." I inched closer to the dark hole. When I peered inside, my heart took up residence in my throat. What in the name of the gods was this?

"Axel!" I hissed. "There's another crystal in there."

"We're barely. Managing. The one. We have!" The strain in Axel's voice made it clear he was seconds away from needing an assist.

"You might want to see this one. It's on a girl."

Axel didn't respond. But a few seconds later, he wrenched his way to my side.

"What do you mean it's on a girl?"

"The crystal." I pointed into the portal. "It's around her neck."

"Torstein!" Axel shouted. "You're going to want to check this out."

"I'm kind of busy," the light mage yelled.

"We'll keep him down." Janna charged at the frost monster. Slashing violently with her sword, she chopped off a chunk of ice from Frosty's forearm. Brigga's dagger removed a frozen finger, while Raynor chipped angrily at the creature's backside.

With the monster distracted, Torstein slogged toward the portal.

"Okay," he grunted. "Now where is this gir —oh. Oh!"

The three of us peered into the darkness. Deep down in the hole, surrounded by a field of snow-covered trees, a small figure jumped up and down. A blue crystal pulsed bright flashes from a string around her neck.

The girl waved her arms overhead and shouted into the air. "Help! Please help me!"

"Is it a trap?" Axel asked. "Is she a frost monster in disguise?"

"I don't think so." Torstein held up his palm. He was probably evaluating her in his peculiar, light-magey way. "But there is something different . . ."

I leaned closer to study the girl. With her cardinal hair and clear, brown eyes, she could easily have passed for a resident of Valkyris. But there was a sadness about her—one that hung palpably across her slightly drooped shoulders. And she was far to weary for her years—she couldn't have been more than eighteen, twenty tops. So why did she look like she'd borne the weight of the world for decades?

*Or centuries?*

My spine stiffened. I had no idea where that thought had come from.

"Torstein?" I hissed. "Are you in my head again?"

"No." Torstein didn't turn around. "You made it clear that was not your preferred method of commu-nication."

I frowned. "I just heard something . . . from *some-where*. And it makes no sense."

"What is it?" Torstein asked.

I glanced over my shoulder. Raynor and Brigga still had the frost monster managed. *For now.*

"Torstein," I whispered. "Ask her when she's from."

"Don't you mean where?"

"No. When."

He turned to look at me. His brows raised as he registered my meaning. "When?"

"Yes," I confirmed.

We all stared into the portal.

"Help!" the girl cried again. "Please save me from this frozen wasteland!"

"Who are you?" Torstein called down.

The girl lowered her arms. "I am Chieftess Bodil of Clan Njord. My people inhabit a fishing village at the southernmost part of the northern territories. I was taken from them . . . some time ago."

*How is this happening?*

Torstein's eyes met mine in an awed stare. "It's her."

"Her, who?" The crack in Axel's voice pulled my attention. I reached over to help him restrain the crystal.

"Her, Bodil," Torstein said. "Sverrir's lost love. The one who was abducted by portal. Her loss is what set him on his dark path."

"She's the girl whose clan lost their magical dagger —the one that was *gifted by the gods*," I whispered.

Axel's nostrils flared. "How is that possible?"

"She's been living for hundreds of years in . . ." Torstein peered into the portal. "Jotunheim? Helheim? The far, far north? It's snowy, but I can't sense whether this is another world, or another time, or—"

"Help! Me!" The girl's panic tugged at my heart. "I don't know how long they'll leave this door open!"

"Get her out of there," I ordered.

"How?" Axel asked.

I stared at Torstein. "Can you extract her? Do one of your magic portal-within-a-portal things?"

Torstein arched one brow. "You have a very high opinion of my capabilities."

"Well? Can you?"

He tilted his head. "As a matter of fact, I can."

He closed his eyes and opened his palm. Angling it into the poral, he moved his hand in a slow circle, then drew it carefully back. The girl rose slowly off the snow. Her body shook as Torstein pulled her above the trees, through a flurry of clouds, and out of the black hole that marked the entrance to our world. Or time. Or . . . whatever this was.

"Be careful," Torstein warned. He lowered her slowly into the water. "Things here are probably very different from what you've grown used to."

The girl clutched the crystal around her neck. Her eyes were wide as they shifted from the cave walls to the fighting Valkyrians to the massive, angry frost monster.

"That beast is the same," she said. "And he isn't going to stay down for long."

"No. I suppose not." Torstein turned his attention to the monster.

"We've been outmaneuvered at every turn. If we had a huge fire, maybe we could melt Frosty down but —oh!" Axel lost his battle with the crystal. It flew from his hands and slammed into the one around Bodil's neck. The two stones stuck together as if they'd fused. Bodil stumbled beneath the additional weight. "I'm sorry, I—"

"Don't apologize." Bodil shifted her necklace. It must have been absurdly heavy, but she kept her head high and spoke with the grace of a chieftess. "My crystal started pulling the moment that door opened. They're clearly two halves of one stone."

"Or two-twelfths," I muttered. I turned back to Torstein. "How do we stop the monster? And close the portal? Axel's right; we're being grossly outmaneuvered. This isn't like the fire monster—then, we had an entire forest at our disposal. Here, we're trapped inside this small cave, with its narrow entrance and an exit that's maybe big enough to fit a dragon, but it's not like we—"

"That's it!" Torstein snapped his fingers together. "Axel. Activate your wrist device."

"Huh?" Axel tore his eyes away from the frost monster struggling to pull free from the whirlpool.

"Summon your dragon," Torstein rephrased. "Bodil's right—this beast *won't* stay down for long. We have to burn him before he gets back up."

Axel reached for the black bracelet he wore around

his wrist. He pushed a button and murmured into the leather, "Rufus. Come."

I stared past the floundering frost monster. Somewhere in the distance was the entrance to the cave. If Rufus was fast then maybe, just maybe, we could pull this off.

If we were *extremely* lucky.

"I've never called for him before," Axel admitted. "Are you sure it will—"

*Whoosh!*

A massive, winged beast swept into the cavern. Its green scales glinted in the light of Torstein's flaming sconces. The creature circled twice, exhaling mighty bursts of fire that lit the ever-shrinking space. The cave had seemed so vast when we'd entered. But now that we shared it with a frost monster and a fire-breathing dragon . . . we needed to put this battle to bed. Fast.

Rufus blew past the frost monster. He tucked his legs to his chest as he sailed over Janna, Brigga, and Raynor. Then, he dropped down and skimmed the surface of the water. A massive wave washed over me, dousing me in its salty spray and nearly pushing me into the portal. Axel reached out to steady me. I held tight to his hand until the tidal wave was no more than a series of sloshes. By then, Rufus was already licking Axel's back. The iguana-turned-dragon proudly thumped his tail against the side of the cave. He seemed to be quite pleased with himself.

"That's it, Rufus. Who's a good boy? Yes, *you're* a good boy." Axel scratched Rufus' chin.

"You have a dragon?" Bodil said breathlessly.

Axel turned to me. "You okay?"

"I'm still on this side of the portal, so *ja*." I grimaced. "I'm doing great."

A fierce roar erupted from the whirlpool. Frosty was slowly clawing his way free. Janna, Brigga and Raynor rushed forward. Their weapons were up, leaving me with no doubt that they'd go at Frosty with everything they had.

But would it be enough?

"Climb aboard." Axel patted Rufus' side. The dragon took a knee, and Axel scaled the shiny, green leg before settling onto Rufus' back.

I paled.

"I'm going to need a second up there," Axel said calmly. "And time is of the essence, so move it, Shieldmaiden."

He held out his hand and I reluctantly let him pull me up.

"I hate flying," I whispered.

"I know you do," he whispered back. "We'll make this fast and painless. Okay?"

I swallowed hard and drew my sword. "Sure thing."

"Rufus. Fly." Axel kicked the dragon with his heels. I threw my shield arm around his waist and held tight as Rufus launched into the air. Axel was a strong rider—the best we had back home. And this wouldn't be nearly as terrifying as my first flight—we couldn't go higher than the cave's ceiling, for one thing. But neither fact stopped the churning in my stomach.

Some of us just weren't meant to fly.

"Stab the monster on our first pass," Axel shouted. His voice was barely discernable over the roar of the wind in my ears. "Aim for his eye, if we can get that close. If we blind him, it gives the ground team a better chance of taking him out."

"Got it." I rotated my sword in a downward-facing grip and waited for Axel's call.

"On my mark . . ." Axel steered the dragon toward our target. "Rufus. Descend!"

Wind blasted my cheeks as the dragon shot toward the ground.

"Flame!" Axel commanded. Fire burst from Rufus' mouth. It enveloped the frost monster, who let out a mighty shriek. "Ingrid, now!"

I slammed my sword arm downward. When it hit its target, a thick, sticky liquid splashed across my arm. I pulled my hand back as Rufus flew away, taking a small amount of pride in the knowledge that Frosty was down one eyeball.

Now to close the deal.

"Circling back!" Axel shouted. He turned Rufus around for a second pass. Below me, my teammates fought for their lives. Between frosty roars came the clang of metal on ice and the woosh of Torstein's light beams. But I didn't allow myself to look. Instead, I kept my focus on my target. As Axel ordered Rufus to dive, then flame, I raised my sword, braced my arm, and struck.

This time, the sticky liquid splattered against my face.

"We got him," I called.

"Good!" Axel yelled back. "One more fire pass should seal it. He's half of his former self."

*Thank gods.*

It took two more flaming flybys to drop the monster to his knees. By that point, our ground team had things well under control. Torstein had stirred another whirlpool—this one holding Frosty firmly in place. Continued blasts from Rufus heated the water enough to melt down the creature's legs. All we needed was one . . . more . . .

"Augh!" My arms shook with the shock of driving my sword into Frosty's head. A resonant *crack* echoed through the cave, and the frost monster's head split neatly in two. It toppled forward, each piece landing on either side of Raynor and sending a massive spray of saltwater splashing up the cave wall. I ducked my head as Axel circled one final time. When we buzzed the headless Frosty, Axel ordered Rufus to strike. The dragon slammed his tail into Frosty's chest, eliciting an explosion that sent ice chunks raining across the cavern. I hurriedly swapped hands, holding Axel's waist with my sword arm and raising my shield to protect us from the razor-sharp shards. When the worst of the shower was over, I carefully lifted my head and took in the scene.

Below us, massive pieces of ice littered the seawa-ter. Torstein dropped his hands, his whirlpool slowing around the now dismantled frost monster. Raynor withdrew his sword from an errant, frosty limb. He reached out to Brigga, who looked up from her furious thigh-jabbing. She stepped back and wiped her brow, relief evident on her delicate features. And near the portal, a shell-shocked Bodil cupped her hand over her mouth.

"Is he really gone?" A tear slipped down her cheek. "Am I . . . finally free?"

"He's dead," Torstein confirmed. The light mage trudged forward, closing the distance between himself and the girl. Axel landed the dragon, and I slid gratefully from its back to plant my feet on solid—albeit watery—ground.

"That was . . ." Brigga exhaled heavily. ". . . something."

"You can say that again," Raynor muttered.

Bodil bent at the waist. She rested her elbows on her knees, breathing heavily. "Thank you. Thank you for getting me out of that . . . that . . ."

"I can only imagine how terrible it was." Torstein glanced at the portal. "But the doorway is still open, and those crystals are a liability. We have to get you to—"

"Augh!" Bodil's spine stiffened as she bolted upright. Her fists clenched into tight balls, and her face pinched in an awkward contortion. She looked to be in unbelievable agony.

"What's happening?" Brigga gasped. "Torstein, help her!"

The light mage leapt forward. His eyes widened as he reached down and pulled something narrow and white from the back of the girl's thigh.

"Bodil," he said carefully. "What do you feel?"

"Pain," she groaned. "It's shooting from my leg into my—oh, gods!" She clutched at her heart. Her fingers crooked and she clawed at her chest. "Get it out!"

"Torstein!" I screamed.

The light mage scooped the girl into his arms. He dropped to a knee, draping Bodil over his leg and cradling her in one arm to keep her head above water. With his other hand, he examined the thing he'd extracted from her thigh.

"What is it?" Janna asked.

"An . . . ice dagger." Torstein closed his eyes. He tightened his grip on the weapon, breathing slowly as he did whatever it was that gave him the knowledge to make his assessment. "It's laced with dark magic."

"What does that mean?" Axel slid off of Rufus' back.

"He said he can't fix dark magic," I said quietly. "He's not going to be able to heal her."

Torstein opened his eyes. He met my gaze, a thousand heartaches locked into one single look. "No," he whispered. "I can't."

Bodil released her hold on her chest. She reached up and cupped Torstein's cheek. "At least I didn't die in that frozen hellscape."

"I'm—I'm sorry." Torstein passed Janna the ice dagger. Then he ran his fingertips along the air beside Bodil's body. When he'd finished, he drew his hand up and snapped his fingers. A white film settled atop the girl's shaking torso. "I can't heal you . . . but I can keep you comfortable until . . ."

"Thank you for freeing me." Bodil's shaking subsided with each ragged breath. "Do you know how long I have to live?"

"I don't," Torstein said sadly. "Dark ailments work in different ways. It could be moments or days."

"I understand." We watched in silence as Bodil struggled to sit. When her eyes locked on the cave's narrow entrance, a faint smile played at her pale lips. She held up one hand, as if trying to reach for something. I followed the line of her pointed finger. A stocky figure stood behind the portal, backlit by the sheen of the distant moon. It moved forward, no more than a shadow until the cave lights shone on his face. Shock colored his jowly features as he approached.

The rest of us drew our weapons.

"Sverrir?" Bodil whispered. "Is it really you?"

The dark mage dropped to his knees. He was still a full dragon-length away. "Bodil?"

"Stand back." Janna jumped in front of the girl. She spoke over her shoulder when she said, "He's dangerous now, Bodil. The darkest mage our world has ever seen. He's trying to destroy everything. We won't let him hurt you."

"My Sverrir would never—" Bodil was overtaken by a raw, rasping cough.

"He would," Torstein said softly. "But we'll protect you."

I stared as the dark mage stalked slowly along the cave wall. His shoulders were tense and his fists balled as he took heavy steps, each producing an angry splash of seawater. His eyes swept from Bodil to Torstein to the black hole before returning to his lost love's crumpled form. Fury flashed in his eyes as he studied the way Torstein hovered over her. I could sense the moment he came to the wrong conclusion.

"Axel," I murmured. "He thinks—"

"You!" His rage-filled face turned on Torstein. "You did this to her!"

"She was struck by a weapon that came from there." Torstein pointed to the portal. "It's laced with dark magic, which you know I cannot heal. But perhaps you could—"

"Dark magic is irreversible!" Sverrir's agonized scream sent chills along my spine.

"We have to get her out of here," I hissed at Axel.

The assassin raised his wrist to his mouth. "Rufus," he whispered into the bracelet. "Move in for a pickup. *Now.*"

The dragon backed up so he stood directly behind us.

"Climb on," Axel ordered. "Brigga, Raynor, Janna, go. Ingrid and I will cover until—"

"Noooo!" Sverrir's rage exploded. He stormed forward, red sparks flying between his fingertips. He turned them on the portal, sending glowing, red lines at its edges. They laced along the perimeter, firing into the darkness before knitting together and tugging the hole closed. While Sverrir worked, I waved my team-mates toward our escape dragon. Janna, Raynor, and Brigga climbed quickly aboard our ride. But the light mage lingered behind.

"Torstein," I hissed. "We have to go. Now."

"Maybe she can stop him from—"

"Now, Torstein. I mean it."

Torstein nodded. He transferred the dual-crystal necklace from Bodil's neck to his own, scooped the girl up in his arms, and carried her onto Rufus. By the time Sverrir had finished with the portal, we were already flying to safety. We raced for the exit, making our way past the rocky arches that guarded the second entrance and soaring up the side of the cliff. I barely dared to breathe as Rufus touched down on the grass, and waited patiently for the six of us to disembark. The second his feet hit the ground, Torstein raised his palms to the compound's perimeter. No doubt he was solidifying its protections to minimize Sverrir's chance of entry. Even so, I wouldn't feel safe until we'd secured the crystals . . . where? Our vault had been compro-mised, our perimeter breached, and we'd left Sverrir more determined than ever to destroy us. By all accounts, we were worse off than we'd been at the day's start.

At least we'd escaped with our lives.

But what if we *didn't* next time? What if Sverrir found us again, and Axel did something stupid—like throwing himself in front of a shot in order to protect us? If Torstein really couldn't heal dark magic, and Axel risked his life to save one of ours . . .

*If I ever lost him . . .*

A fierce tremor wracked my body as I tried to shake the thought free. I had enough to worry about without dwelling on what-ifs. Like how we could possibly keep our newfound crystals safe.

And what were we going to do with the dying love of our dark mage's life?

## CHAPTER 10

WHILE TORSTEIN, JANNA AND Axel took care of our crystals, Brigga and I explained our situation to Bodil. We'd settled her into a guest cottage. The multi-talented Magnus had been tasked with nurse duty, and Raynor helped him set up a series of medical apparatus Magnus claimed would monitor Bodil's vital signs. While they worked, Brigga and I plumped pillows, prepared tea, and arranged a tray with fruits, breads, and meat.

"You must be hungry," Brigga urged. "Eat something so you have some energy."

"I'm not sure what good it would do," Bodil said sadly. "I just hope I can use what time I have left to help Sverrir change his course. Did that mage . . . Torstar?"

"Torstein," I corrected as I slipped another pillow beneath her head. She lay calmly in the large bed by the window, surrounded by white bedding. She looked even paler than she'd been in the cave.

"Did Torstein say my Sverrir is going to destroy the world?"

"He's trying." Brigga grimaced. We quickly filled Bodil in on the man Sverrir had become after she'd disappeared.

"I can't believe . . ." Bodil shook her head. "No matter. I *will* do all I can to help you stop him. I won't have him remembered as the darkest mage to ever grace this earth."

"We could use all the help we can get," I admitted. "But I'm afraid Sverrir is a lost cause. Your energy would be better spent focusing on healing."

"Torstein said I can't be healed." Bodil didn't blink. "But I'll eat. The longer I hold out, the more I can be of use."

"I don't understand." I buttered a slice of bread and passed it over. "How could you love someone who's so . . ."

"Evil?" Brigga added softly.

I shot her an admonishing look. "Shh!"

"He wasn't always like this." Bodil took the tiniest of bites. After centuries in an ice prison, did she really have the appetite of a bird? "He was so kind when I knew him. Honest. Virtuous. He wanted only the best for the people he loved, and he'd have done anything in his power to see that they got it."

"That's not the Sverrir we know." I poured water into a glass and set it on the table beside the bed. "I'm sorry—this must all come as such a shock."

"Pain changes people." Bodil took another nibble

of bread. "There were many times when I thought I'd lose my mind in that frozen nightmare. But I thought of Sverrir often . . . I knew he'd want me to be strong."

Bodil struggled to sit up, reaching for the water glass with a trembling arm. I quickly lifted it for her and brought it to her lips.

"Thanks," she said gratefully. When she'd taken a sip, I set the glass back on the table.

"Are you all right?" I asked.

"I'm sad for what Sverrir's become," she said honestly. "He was a good man once. And even if he can't be that man anymore, I know a part of him still remembers who he truly is. Hopefully, I can help you reach that"—her arms stretched overhead as she let out a big yawn—"that part of him."

Brigga and I exchanged a look. I quickly moved the tray to the bedside table while Brigga pulled the comforter over Bodil's chest. "You must be exhausted," Brigga said. "We'll leave the food here and let you rest. Just call for us if there's anything that you need."

"Thank you." Bodil yawned again. "You're all so kind."

I tiptoed toward the door with Brigga close on my heels. By the time we stepped into the cottage's living area, Bodil was already snoring gently.

Raynor and Magnus looked up from the couch where they were fidgeting with a large, illuminated box.

"How is she?" Raynor asked.

"Exhausted," I said. "But she doesn't seem to be in pain."

"Torstein took care of that," Brigga said. "And Magnus, you'll let us know if anything changes?"

The assistant nodded briskly. "I will report to Torstein should the patient's status change. I presume he'll keep you apprised."

"I'm sure he will." I dropped into the chair beside the window, trying not to think about everything Bodil had been through. Of how she'd been ripped away from her love; been kept apart from half of her heart for so many years. Her pain must have been overwhelming. A shiver surged along my spine as fear raced through me. If I'd been in her shoes, would I have been able to stay strong? Now that I knew what it was to be with Axel, if anything were to ever happen to him . . .

*How could I possibly survive?*

I closed my eyes and rubbed my temples. It had been a long night.

And gods only knew what the day would bring.

The sun had just peeked over the skyline of Los Angeles when Torstein dropped us off on The Row. Exhaustion blurred the edges of my consciousness as I stumbled up the steps of Kappa Mu and struggled to forget the sheer volume of atrocities I'd experienced in the past ten hours. Not only had we battled a frost monster, recovered two crystals, rescued a thousand-plus-year-old chieftess, and set a dark mage on an even darker path, but we'd managed a minor dragon malfunction. Axel had found himself unable to shrink Rufus back to his standard iguana size. And Torstein was so drained from the evening's events, he needed a nap before fixing Axel's wrist controller. Our mage had taken the bracelet, promising to fix it by the day's end. Then he'd driven us home before heading back to his compound, where he'd hidden a full-sized Rufus inside a hastily constructed tent.

Gods willing, the dragon stayed put.

We slugged past a perky-eyed Kenzi, apologized for skipping yoga—*again*—and plopped facedown our beds. My eyes were so heavy that I didn't even untie my boots before I passed out.

It was going to be a long day.

## CHAPTER 11

W E SLEPT STRAIGHT THROUGH our morning class. Morgan had knocked on our door before she left, but I mumbled something about food poisoning and she'd promised to bring us her notes. By early afternoon, we'd pulled ourselves together enough to nurse steaming mugs in the Kappa Mu dining room. I was on my second coffee—and already feeling the caffeine-induced jitters—when a mini-skirt-wearing mean girl sauntered down the steps. Lexi cast a disparaging look around the room. When her eyes settled on me, she arched one brow, jutted her hip, and strolled toward our table. Her face sparked with ill-contained triumph, and I took another hit of my beverage to summon both strength and grace.

Frigga knew, I was going to need it.

None of us addressed Lexi when she positioned herself in front of our table. Instead, we raised our mugs to our lips and drank.

*Patience,* I prayed. *Gods give me patience.*

"Well?" Lexi placed one hand on her hip.

I continued sipping my coffee.

"Aren't you going to defend yourselves?" she pressed.

Janna sighed loudly. "For what, exactly?"

Lexi's nostrils flared. "The three of you stayed out *all night.* That is conduct unbecoming of a sister and an automatic demerit."

"What makes you think we stayed out all night?" I asked.

"I saw you come in, *Inga.*" Lexi said not-my-name as if it were a dirty word. "That same hot driver that you left with last night dropped you off at sunrise."

So she was familiar with Torstein.

My gaze slid over to Janna. She shrugged. "We stayed out. We accept the demerit. Now please move so I can get another cup of—"

"Hi there, ladies." A smiling Meri strolled up to our table. "What are you up to to—oh." Her gaze moved from Janna to Lexi to me and back. "Not again," Meri groaned. "Lexi, what's your problem this time?'

"Why do you automatically assume I have a problem?" Lexi asked.

"Because we've done this dance *way* too many times." Meri crossed her arms.

Lexi lifted her chin. "For your information, these three stayed out all night. I've issued a demerit for their infraction, but I think leadership should take a long look at whether our *guests* are accurately upholding the values we revere in this sorority."

Meri rolled her eyes. "Lexi. You've stayed out plenty of times."

Lexi's mouth flapped open. "I have not!"

"Just because you don't write yourself up doesn't mean the rest of us don't see what you do." Meri shook her head. "Not that we care—you're only young once, right? And so long as you're not hurting anyone, I give zero hoots what you do with your free time."

I took a slow drag on my coffee. This was getting good.

"Well, I do care. And these three are making our house look bad to the rest of the Row. Automatic demerits have been issued." Lexi looked as if she'd just won a tournament.

Meri looked at Janna. "Did you guys break curfew?"

"We did," Janna admitted. "We accept our punishment."

My captain was far too honorable to lie—unless it was a professional necessity, of course.

"That's very honest of you." Meri uncrossed her arms. "And this house has always respected honesty. Which is why we offer a work-off system for minor-infraction demerits. Did Lexi tell you about that?"

I arched my eyebrows and stared at Lexi. "She did not."

"Oh, come on!" Lexi huffed.

"I'm making my grandmother's potato lefse for the senior center." Meri pointed to the kitchen. "I bake for all the big Scandinavian holidays, and since Saint Lucia's is this weekend, I'm dropping off a batch a few days early. If you want to help me, you can work off your demerit."

Brigga put down her mug. "We'd love to."

"Thanks, Meri," Janna said.

Lexi turned on one heel and stormed angrily away.

"Seems like that's settled." Meri rubbed her hands together. "Shall we?"

I picked up my mug and crossed to the beverage table for another refill. Then I followed my friends into the kitchen, tied on an apron, and washed my hands.

"Where are the potatoes?" Brigga asked.

"Mmm?" Meri pulled a black-footed pan from the cupboard. She unknotted its cord, and plugged it into the wall. Then, she crossed the pantry and pulled out a bag of flour. "Oh, I'm not using potatoes."

"I thought you said you were making your grand-mother's potato lefse?" I walked to the counter.

"I am." Meri grinned. "She makes it with *instant* potatoes."

What the Helheim was an instant potato?

"We've never, uh, done it that way." Janna shot me a curious look.

"It's *super* easy. I actually mixed half the dough yesterday, so I could cook it today. That way I'm not flipping lefse for hours and hours." Meri rubbed her arm with a laugh.

"Sounds good." Brigga pushed up her sleeves. "Where do we start?"

Meri pulled several baking dishes from the refrigerator. "These are ready to be cooked. One of you can roll out the balls, one can cook the lefse, and one can help me mix up the new batch. Anybody have a preference?"

"I'll roll," Brigga offered.

"I'll cook," Janna chimed in.

"Guess I'll mix." I moved to stand beside Meri. We'd planned to make her grandmother's lefse with her a few weeks back, but life—and the mission—had intervened. "I've never done it this way—we use flour back home."

"Hardangerlefse? I love that version." Meri passed me a massive bowl and a mixing spoon. "Your arms look stronger than mine. You can mix."

"Deal." I looked around. "Where's the recipe?"

Meri tapped her head. "Up here. Ingrid, go ahead and put five cups of water on the stove to boil. Janna and Brigga, I'll show you how to roll out the dough."

I crossed to the big island countertop and reached overhead. After pulling down a copper pot, I moved to the sink and filled it with water. While I fumbled with the stove, Meri demonstrated the proper rolling technique.

"Use plenty of flour on your mat." She sprinkled a healthy portion of white dust onto the counter. "And be sure to use some on your rolling pin—it keeps the dough from sticking."

"You want them to be thin?" Janna's brow was furrowed in concentration. I didn't know much about my captain's pre-shieldmaiden life, but I guessed that she hadn't spent much—if any—time baking.

"Within reason," Meri said. "We don't want them to tear when we pick them up."

"Right." Janna got to rolling.

"Brigga, have you flipped lefse before?" Meri asked.

"Yes, but not on one of these." Brigga eyed the black-footed cooking circle.

"I *love* this pan. But it does tend to stick, so be sure to spray a light layer of oil every now and then." Meri picked up a cylinder labeled *cooking spray* and pressed down on its top. A thin burst of liquid shot at the circle. "I like to wait until bubbles form to flip my lefse, but if you have your own system, use that. I'm sure it's great."

She handed Brigga a long wooden flipping stick, then picked up a box labeled *waxed paper.*

"I also ball up some of this and dust the excess flour from the pan—keeps those burn marks at a minimum, and prevents the taste from being compromised."

"Thanks, Meri." Brigga stared. "That's a good tip."

No doubt our disseminator was trying to figure out how to bring the box home for reproduction.

"Okay, Ingrid." Meri grabbed another copper pot from the top of the island. "Let's get mixing."

Meri added butter and salt to the boiling water before handing me an enormous box labeled *instant mashed potatoes.* As I dumped the dried flakes into my bowl, Meri stirred the pot.

"Do you do this often?" I asked. "Make big lefse batches to donate?"

"I make dishes for all the big holidays," Meri said. "The seniors love it. I do waffles for Syttende Mai, lefse for Saint Lucia, kransekake for Midsommers . . ."

"You must be a really accomplished baker." Brigga looked over. "Kransekake is hard."

"I make it every Christmas with my grandmother." Meri tapped her wooden spoon on the pot. "We should make that together too—before I leave for winter break."

If we were still here at winter break, the world would be in all kinds of trouble.

"How will you be spending your time off?" Janna asked.

"I'm going home to Minnesota. Hopefully my plane doesn't get a snow delay this year."

I glanced at Janna. We'd learned the giant metal dragons were *planes* . . . after we'd referred to them otherwise, then been forced to pretend we'd been joking.

"My family always comes over for a huge Christmas Eve celebration," Meri said as she poured the contents of the pot into my bowl. "My cousins and I spend the entire day baking with Grandma, and then we try not to eat it all before the actual feast. If we're lucky, a few of the dishes survive."

My spoon made slow work through the dried potato, butter and water mixture. "It sounds like a fun tradition

"It is." Meri added milk to my bowl. "Plus, we take plenty of sledding breaks. There's never a lack of snow back home, and we always have a snowman-building contest after the big sled races. Girl cousins versus boy cousins. The girls usually win."

"As they should," Janna said seriously. "We do similar winter solstice competitions back home. Ours are ski races, but the boys haven't won a match in five years, so maybe we should offer them a sledding option."

I bit back my smile. Janna had told me the shield-maidens' record was impressive, but I hadn't realized we'd held our streak for quite so long. I'd definitely be brushing up on my cross-country when we got back to Valkyris. I didn't want to bring shame to my squadron.

*Let's just focus on having a Valkyris to get back to.*

Sigh.

"Sledding is great." Meri put the milk back in the refrigerator. "Even my grandma gets in on it. She's eighty going on eighteen. Her motto is, 'Always say yes to adventure.'"

"She sounds wonderful," Brigga said.

"She is. We talk every week, and we send funny e-mails back and forth. She's the only person in the world I'll watch one of those dumb cat videos for. But they just crack her up!" Meri laughed. "I guess they kind of crack me up, too."

I had no idea what a cat video was. Thankfully, Meri kept talking.

"She came to America all by herself—her family

owned a business in Norway, but she wanted to see the world before she settled down, so she got a job as a stewardess. She fell in love with an air traffic controller she met at the Minneapolis airport, they got married, and here we all are."

My forearm burned as I continued turning my spoon.

"That must have been scary for her," Brigga said. "Moving somewhere all alone."

"I'm sure it was at first," Meri said. "But as time went on, she built a family for herself. She had my grandpa, and she was very involved in their church. Some of the ladies there were immigrants, too, and they formed a pretty tight group. They looked after each other's kids, and celebrated the holidays together, and went camping in the summers. Grandma always says her found family is every bit as important to her as the one she was born into."

A smile tugged at my lips. I could certainly relate to that. My squadron, my friends in Valkyris, Axel— they'd grown to occupy more space in my heart than I'd ever thought possible. I hadn't always had the most secure life, but now I had a place and a purpose worth fighting for. Family, no matter how you came to it, was everything. And I would do everything in my power to protect the one I'd come to be a part of. Because family was worth any risk. *Love* was worth any risk.

*Wasn't it?*

"Well done, Ingrid." Meri interrupted my thoughts. "I'd say that dough is mixed enough. Now we mold them into little balls and place them in covered baking dishes. We'll leave these to chill overnight. I can roll them out tomorrow."

"How big do you want them to be?" I took a fistful of dough in one hand, and shaped it into a sphere. "Does this work?"

"That's perfect," Meri said. "You've done this before?"

"A few times," I said. The recipe may have changed, but it was nice to know some traditions had lasted through the centuries.

The chime of the doorbell made me look up.

"I'll get that." Meri dusted her hands on her apron. "You two doing okay over there?"

"We're nearly finished," Brigga confirmed. Beside her was an enormous stack of neatly folded lefse.

"Wonderful! I can run that batch over to the center this afternoon. Thanks for the help." Meri slipped out of the kitchen. I finished rolling out my dough, then placed it in the refrigerator. As I closed the door, Meri called out. "Ingrid! Your boyfriend's here!"

I quickly washed my hands, and dried them on my apron. Since boys weren't allowed beyond the dining room steps, I hurried out of the kitchen to meet my visitor.

"*Hei*," I said as I stepped into the entryway. "Long time no see."

"Nice apron." Axel's gaze roamed up and down my body. "I've never seen you in that look before."

"Hey." I swatted him. "I can cook."

"I never said you couldn't." He paused. "Though you've never done it for me, so . . ."

My fist landed squarely in his bicep.

Meri chuckled. "I'll leave you two alone. Good to see you, Axel."

"You too." Axel rubbed his arm. Once Meri was gone, the smile dropped from his face. "We need to get out of here."

My muscles tensed. "Why? What's happened?"

"Nothing bad," he assured me. "It's good, actually."

"Well?" My stomach churned.

"Torstein's outside with the car."

"Oh, gods." I groaned. "What now?"

"He got a read on Sverrir last night. During that moment right before"—he lowered his voice—"we found Bodil."

"How is she doing?" I asked quietly.

"Torstein says she's comfortable . . . but he doesn't think she has long. She hasn't been up to talking much, but she has managed to brief him on her history with the dark mage."

"I know she wants us to reach him. I just don't think he's redeemable."

Axel frowned. "Neither do I."

"So, what happened last night? How did Torstein get a read on him?"

"Sverrir's defenses dropped enough for Torstein to pick up on his thoughts, or . . . whatever it is that he does." Axel shook his head. "Anyway, he saw that

Sverrir *is still looking* for the balboa. He hasn't found it yet."

*Oh, thank gods.* "That's great."

"That's more than great," Axel said. "It means we have a chance to locate and destroy it before he can collect it. And if we do that—"

"Then he can't do the spell, and he can't destroy Valkyris." I wrung my hands together. It was too much to hope for.

"We have to act fast. How soon can you get out of here?"

I glanced over my shoulder. "We're just finishing up baking lefse."

Axel didn't bat an eye. "Bring some of that with you."

"It's for the senior citizens."

"Oh. Well . . ." His lips turned down. He looked like somebody had just taken away his prized dragon.

"I'll see what I can do," I amended. "Give us fifteen minutes to clean up and change."

"I'll meet you in the car. I'll be the one holding the broadsword."

He leaned down to brush my forehead with his lips. Then he turned for the door and let himself out. With each step, the muscles of his backside flexed beneath his fitted pants. Not that I was staring at Axel's butt. I was a girl on a mission—focused, determined . . .

And not the *slightest* bit distracted.

*Snort.*

# CHAPTER 12

F OR ONCE, TRAFFIC WAS light. We made it out of Los Angeles in record time, and followed the freeway signs to San Diego. A light rain broke out as we drove, leaving the roads slick and our fellow drivers extra cautious. Apparently, *weather* was a liability in the sunny, coastal region.

*Good thing they don't live in Norway.*

Torstein slowed as he pulled into a crowded lot. We passed a sign reading "Welcome to Balboa Park," then pulled into a space at the back of the parking area. There were fewer cars here . . . though still more than I'd expected for a weekday afternoon.

"Don't these people have jobs?" Axel muttered.

"Most of them seem to be children." Brigga pointed out of her window. "Well, children and their guardians. This must be a popular family place."

"Of course it is." Raynor stared out the window. "So, what's our play?"

"We don't exactly have one. When I was here before, I didn't pick up on anything. We're shooting in the dark." Torstein stepped out of the car. The rest of us followed.

I stretched my arms overhead, tilting my face to the sky so the rain misted my cheeks. It was hardly a downpour—nothing like what we were used to back home. But the dim sky and heavy clouds must have been off-putting to our fellow visitors. A steady stream of parents and children made their way across the lot. They climbed into their cars and fled the not-a-storm.

"Well, that helps," I said.

"Mmm." Axel studied the area. "This place is huge. What's the layout?"

"I grabbed a map the last time I was here." Torstein reached into the car. He pulled a piece of parchment from the box between the front seats. He opened it up, and we all gathered around. "The zoo occupies the largest piece of land. Off of that are the theatres—one's old-fashioned, the other more modern. There are several museums—those are here, here, and here." He pointed. "The archery range is over there."

Axel's head whipped up. "They have archers?"

"Recreational ones," Torstein explained. "Their warriors don't train in this park. They have a facility located closer to the ocean."

"Oh." Axel's shoulders relaxed.

"Then there are the gardens—the Botanical Garden, Japanese Friendship Garden, Cactus Garden—"

"It has to be in one of the gardens," Brigga said confidently.

"I searched them before," Torstein said. "None emitted so much as a trace of magic."

Brigga's face fell. "Oh."

"Who said the tree was magic?" Raynor asked.

"Our professor, for one," Janna pointed out. "Balboa bark is supposed to contain properties similar to the fountain of youth. No purely organic substance could keep someone young."

"Unless it could." Brigga's lips formed a pert O. "Think about it. Kenzi's always talking about green tea, and fish oil, and flaxseed, and those weird mushrooms she gets at the farmer's market. What if this balboa is like those things . . . just amplified?"

"I never thought of that," Torstein admitted. "If that's the case, we need to search the entire area on foot. This park has countless gardens—scanning it for organic matter won't narrow down much."

I searched the recesses of my mind. "Professor Clark said the balboa grew wilder than the other plants. We're going to be looking for something that's unruly."

"And well hidden," Brigga added. "He also said nobody's found it—not in modern history, anyway."

"So it can't be that big." I steepled my fingertips together. "Hmm. A well-hidden, smallish, wild-growing plant. Where could that be concealed for hundreds of years?"

"Unless it's been moved, it has to be outside. That rules out the museums," Janna said.

"And the theatres," Raynor added.

"And the science center." Axel looked up from the map.

"I think it's in one of the gardens," Brigga reiterated. "Hidden in plain sight."

"There are a *lot* of gardens." Janna frowned. "Rose Garden. Cactus Garden. Japanese Friendship Garden. Botanical Garden. Alcazar Garden. Zoro Garden."

"Which one of those is most likely to hide a maybe-magical plant?" I asked.

Torstein closed his eyes. He was silent for a long time. When he finally spoke, he uttered a single word. "Cactus."

"What?" Axel asked.

"Cactus." Torstein's eyes opened. "Southwestern cultures have revered the cactus for hundreds of years. It is used in religious ceremonies, cultivated in rituals, and certain species *are* believed to have magical properties—including the extension of youth. If someone wanted the balboa to blend in, a cactus garden would be the perfect place to hide it."

Axel turned toward the green space behind us. "Then that's where we'll go."

Raynor peered at the map. "That's the Alcazar Garden. The Cactus Garden is over *there*."

Axel turned the other way. "Right."

"You heard him." Janna crossed to the trunk and passed out our weapons. "And remember, if anyone asks about our weapons, we're carrying them because we are in a play."

"Think that'll work here, too?" I hooked my shield onto my back.

"I have no idea," she said honestly. "But we're about to find out."

Two hours later, water poured freely from the sky. Wet clothes clung to my skin, and my thick head of hair hung heavily down my back. We'd combed nearly every inch of the dirt-lined trails. As we rounded the final corner, the weight of desolation filled my heart. Our window was closing. The alignment was just days away, and Sverrir had collected nearly everything he needed to do the unthinkable. We had this small opportunity remaining to thwart him, and if we failed again . . .

*Stop it, Ingrid. Failure is* not *an option.*

But it was a possibility.

"I don't see anything." Janna dropped onto a bench. She lowered her head to her hands.

"I do," Brigga whispered. Her eyes shone with excitement as she bounced lightly on her toes. She jabbed one pointed finger at the low hill behind the path. "Look!"

"All I see are a *lot* of cactuses. The same ones we've walked past for—"

"No, Raynor. *Look.*" Brigga walked up the hill. When

she was halfway to the top, she dropped to her knees and held out her hand. "See it?"

I squinted through the rain. "All I see is a clump of saguaros. Or are those prickly pears? I lost track of the names twenty spiky species' ago."

Brigga let out an exasperated sigh. "Just get up here, will you?"

I held out my hand and pulled Janna to her feet. "After you, Captain."

She drew her shoulders back. "Onward?"

"And upward," I confirmed. Together we marched over the rocks, sidestepped needle-laden arms, and avoided fallen blooms. When we reached Brigga, I studied the cluster of cacti. The tight circle of dark green trunks gave way to a sea of upwardly reaching branches. They wove together, creating a plant-made shield that appeared impenetrable to all but the smallest of birds. *Or rodents.* I eyed the tiny mouse dodging raindrops as it scurried into the cover of the dome. Inside, there was *another* plant. I had to duck down and squint to see between the lower, more widely spaced branches. But the outer plants were hiding something that almost looked like . . .

"What is that thing?" Axel stepped forward.

Brigga looked up triumphantly. "A low-lying, unwieldly bush/shrub being concealed by an army of spiky guards."

I studied the obscured plant. It was well hidden from the main path—and barely visible even at close range. But as I peered between the guard cacti's posts, I made out its thick, green trunk, wildly winding limbs, and needle-free branches that entwined while reaching outward like crooked, craggy fingers.

It looked like something straight out of a nightmare.

"It does fit the description," Janna agreed. "But how will we know if it's our target? Didn't Professor Clark say something about the *real* balboa shedding magic-encrusted bark beneath the full moon?"

I glanced at the cloud-covered sky. "We won't see a moon tonight."

"We don't need to," Torstein said. He crouched down and reached out his hand. A faint white mist immediately surrounded the cluster, then seeped through the cracks to drape over the mystery plant. Torstein was "reading" it.

*What does he see?*

"Well?" I glanced nervously toward the path. Nobody was walking toward us. And the only groundskeeper in sight was driving a curious-looking vehicle a fair distance away. *Thank gods.*

"It doesn't hold any magic," Torstein said. "But we decided that it didn't have to—there are natural ways to extend youthfulness. This one is definitely older than the rest of the surrounding plants—*much* older. Its roots seem to go back at least three hundred years."

Axel let out a low whistle. "So it's a contender."

"Look down," I suggested. "Are there any bark drop-pings inside that circle?"

Brigga peered through the narrow gap in the

branches. "There's something," she confirmed. "Could be pieces of bark. Could be a nest—ew, that's some big poop. What kind of animal is small enough to squeeze through these trunks and still make a mess that big?"

"Ferret," I offered, at the same time as Torstein said, "Raccoon."

"What?" He raised his shoulders at my quizzical glance. "Raccoons are diggers. They're in the trash at our fraternity all the time. One might have burrowed—check for a hole—and a gap in the roots."

"What's a raccoon?" Janna whispered.

"No idea," I said. Then I turned to Brigga. "So, is there bark on the ground?"

"I think so," Brigga said tentatively.

"Let me run a few scans," Torstein said. "See what I can identify."

We huddled around our light mage, careful to obscure him from view. Not that there was anyone nearby—the only other visitors were all the way up at the entrance. Three small children splashed in a big puddle, while an elderly couple watched them from beneath the shelter of an awning.

While Torstein worked, I wrung the rain from my hair and pulled my curls back in a loose braid. The shorter strands around my face refused to be tamed, so I let them cling to my temples as I turned my attention to the perimeter. The children continued to charm the older couple—their grandparents? Just beyond the park's boundary, a determined jogger ran along the path. Cars drove on the distant road, too far away to pay us any attention. By all accounts, we were secure.

"This is the plant we've been looking for." Torstein's declaration jarred me from my assessment. Relief and excitement coursed through me, the dueling emotions causing my torso to fold in on itself at the same time my toes tapped a happy rhythm. "It's at least twice as old as the rest of the plants in this park, but its exterior is only three-and-a-half weeks old. The topcoat was shed on the date of the last full moon. I don't know how it keeps humans young, but its trunk definitely contains rejuvenating properties."

Hope bubbled in my heart. "That's great. Now, how do we get it out of here?"

"Can you port it out?" Axel asked.

"No," Torstein said. "If Sverrir's watching, any use of magic will alert him to our location. I'm worried that he may have already detected me, just from my scanning it. If we want to extract this thing, we need to do it through physical means."

"And we need to do it without anyone noticing." Brigga wrung her hands together. "I read that this park is protected land, and removal of *any* natural object is a crime punishable by imprisonment."

"*Ja*, well, not removing this object could result in the end of the world," Axel countered.

Brigga's brows knitted together. "I wonder . . ."

"What are you thinking?" I asked.

Her gaze swept the property. "Do you think the groundskeepers keep their uniforms on-site?"

Recognition flickered across my brain. "Brigga, that's brilliant. I saw one of their trucks drive by earlier."

"You're going to have to fill the rest of us in," Raynor said.

"If we dress up as gardeners and say we're removing a sick plant to avoid the spread of infection, we can extract the balboa without raising suspicion," I said excitedly.

"And you think you can just waltz into their offices, borrow an outfit, and steal a magic plant?" Raynor asked.

"No." Brigga put her hands on Raynor's arms. "But you can."

Twenty minutes later, Axel and Raynor squirmed uncomfortably in their uniforms.

"Mine is too short." Raynor tugged at the one-piece suit.

"I grabbed what I could," Torstein said apologetically. "These were the only three in lockers."

"It's definitely tight." Axel pulled down his sleeves. "But then, most people aren't as muscular me."

I patted his shoulder. "Way to stay humble, Andersson."

"What? It's true."

I squeezed his arm. He wasn't wrong.

"Okay. Everyone clear on your responsibilities?" Torstein addressed our team.

"Janna and I will redirect any foot traffic," I said. "You, Axel and Raynor will dig up the balboa. And Brigga is our lookout—if something comes up, she'll signal us from the top of the hill."

"Correct." Torstein folded his hands together. "Once the plant is out, we'll load it into the truck and drive it back to my vehicle. Once we load it up, we can bring it back to the compound and dispose of it."

Brigga hesitated. "We're going to destroy the fountain of youth?"

"There's no confirmation it was ever used for that," I pointed out. "Professor Clark said it was only a legend."

"And legends exist for a reason," she countered.

"In this case, I think the importance of destruction outweighs the benefits of preservation," Torstein said gently. "Remember, if Sverrir gets his hands on this—"

"I know," Brigga groaned. "I just . . . this meant a lot to a lot of people."

"Sometimes in battle we have to make hard calls," Janna said quietly. "I'm afraid this is one of them."

Brigga sighed. "I know."

I leaned toward her. "If it helps, I feel bad too."

She offered me a tight smile. "Thanks."

"Okay. Everyone to your places." Axel clapped his hands. "The faster we do this, the better."

We got straight to work. Torstein backed the truck to the edge of the path while Axel and Raynor dug toward the back of the cactus dome. Brigga whistled softly, and Janna and I followed her sightline to the bend in the path. A young couple walked hand in hand through the rain, apparently too blinded by love to be deterred by the downpour.

Janna and I hustled along the path.

"Whew!" I exclaimed loudly as we neared the couple. "That section of the park was a *mess.*"

"You're telling me." Janna flicked water from her sleeve. "Maintenance cannot clear it out fast enough."

The girl tilted her head. "Are they working back there?"

"A crew is clearing the walkway," I lied. "It's flooded."

"Really?" The boy frowned. "I thought this park was specifically landscaped to maximize rain flow so that flooding wasn't an issu—"

"There was an accident," I blurted. "One of the trucks dropped some, uh, planters on the path. They damaged the pavement and messed up the flow."

"Oh." The girl winced. "That's bad."

"There's mud and water *everywhere*," I said dramatically. "I'd turn back if I were you."

"Thanks for the tip." The girl's gaze swept from my sheathed sword to the shield strapped to my back. "Are the two of you lost? You look like you belong at the Old Globe."

"Huh?"

"The theatre around the way," she said. "You're dressed for Shakespeare."

*Right!*

"Yes." I nodded solemnly. "We were just taking a break from practicing our theatre . . . thing."

"I knew it. Break a leg!" The girl turned around. "Come on, Arthur. I was getting cold anyway."

"Let me warm you up." He slung his arm around her shoulders.

As they left, Janna crossed her arms. "That was easy enough."

"Sure was." I looked up to where Brigga silently scanned the park. "I wonder how the guys are doing. I'd imagine this could take quite a while."

Brigga waved both hands and jumped up and down.

"Or not." Janna moved backwards. "Looks like they're all done."

We jogged along the path. When we reached the truck, we unclipped our shields and lay them in the bed. Then we jumped in after them and tucked ourselves under a waterlogged tarp. Torstein climbed into the driver's seat while Axel and Raynor loaded the wild-looking plant on top of our shields.

"Careful," Raynor warned as Brigga scooted in behind me. "There aren't any needles, but some of the branches are awfully spiky."

"I'll try not to touch it," she promised. "Just get us out of here. I'm cold."

Raynor closed the back hatch, then followed Axel inside the truck. Seconds later, we bumped along the pavement on our way to the parking lot.

"I hope Torstein can explain his way out of here," Janna said quietly.

"He'll think of something," I whispered back. "He always does."

The truck slowed to a stop. *Here we go.*

"Excuse me," a deep male voice boomed. "Do you have an authorization for this transport?"

"Just taking a sick plant off-site for rehabilitation," Torstein said calmly.

Papers shuffled. "I don't see an order for that."

"It was a last-minute request. They're probably still filling out the order." Torstein sounded apologetic. "The damage in this one spread so quickly, the director was worried about it infecting other species. And since it was in a protected enclave. . ."

"Yes. Well." The man didn't sound happy. "Make sure the order gets put through. I don't want to get in trouble."

"Of course," Torstein said.

"Move along." The man grunted.

I didn't exhale until the truck bumped forward. *Thank gods that worked.*

We drove for a while, with Janna, Brigga and I bunched together beneath the blue tarp. The parking lot was a fair distance from the Cactus Garden—which was good, since it got us well out of view of the guards. But it wasn't so great on my back. In the several minutes it took to reach Torstein's SUV, I rolled into Brigga, Janna, *and* the spiky plant more times than I cared to count.

When we finally came to a stop, the truck's doors creaked open. After a moment, Axel lifted the fabric and shot me a grin.

"Made it." He moved to the waiting SUV, and opened the trunk.

"Thank gods." I uncurled my legs, and climbed unsteadily from the back of the groundskeeper's vehicle. The lot was deserted. Only a handful of cars remained, and their owners were nowhere to be seen. *Whew.* "Now, let's get this thing out of here and get rid of it already."

"There's nothing I'd rather—"

"Uff!" Air rushed from my lungs as Axel's thick arm hit my chest. I flew backwards, slamming into the back of a nearby car while chaos erupted around me. Janna jumped out of the truck, Brigga climbed unsteadily after her, and Raynor raised his blade in front of the stolen balboa. Meanwhile, Torstein tossed a sparking ball between his outstretched hands.

"What the Helheim is happening?" I shouted.

"Just stay back!" Axel yelled.

*Ja. Right.*

I drew my sword. My shield was still in the truck, but I'd been down a weapon before. Only this time, I couldn't see what we were fighting.

"Just get the balboa into my car," Torstein yelled. "I can't see him, but I can feel him."

"Him who?" Janna raised her blade. Then she swore. Loudly.

My heart froze as a small, black disc appeared

173

above the truck. It expanded until it was the size of a door, then shook violently. The air around us crackled, and a gust of wind sent me flying onto my backside. By the time I'd managed to stand, the hole had disappeared.

And the balboa along with it.

Axel and Raynor swore in tandem. Janna slammed her fist into her thigh. And our normally stoic light mage let loose with a shout of frustration that sent a nearby cluster of trash-eating seagulls soaring for the skies.

*Holy. Mother. Frigga.*

"Is it . . ." Brigga peeked into the bed.

"Gone," Janna confirmed.

"How?" I asked. "It had to be Sverrir, but Torstein didn't use magic. We didn't see him following us. How did he come from out of nowhere and suck an object right out from under us?"

"That's what he does." Torstein cradled his head in his hands. "I was on my guard, but he still managed to . . ."

"Hey." I sheathed my sword and walked to his side. "You did your best. We all did."

"And yet, here we are. Again." Torstein's eyes were bottomless pools of pain.

"Is this it?" Brigga asked timidly. "Is it over now?"

"It's not over until he gets the dagger," I swore, "which he'll *never* do. I will die before I let him get his hands on Freia's blade."

"And *I* will die before I let anything happen to you," Axel vowed.

Worry churned in my gut. I had no doubt my boyfriend would make good on that promise. But I couldn't have him putting himself in danger for me. If he did, and if anything were to happen . . .

*Don't go there, Ingrid. This is* not *the time to fall apart.*

As I looked into Axel's eyes, I knew he was thinking what neither of us wanted to say. Things were bad. *Very bad.*

It would take a miracle to save Valkyris now.

## CHAPTER 13

S ATURDAY CAME MUCH TOO quickly. We all knew the winter formal would be our last hope. In a little more than twelve hours, the planets would align, the crystals would re-charge, and Sverrir would have his chance to destroy everything we'd worked to build. The only thing standing between us and total annihilation was the magical dagger strapped to my back . . . which meant that as much as this mission was a team effort, *I* was the last line of defense—for the future of Valkyris, and the lives of my friends.

*Just. Don't. Blow it.*

With so much riding on tonight, Janna, Brigga, and I opted out of taking the Kappa Mu bus to San Diego. Instead, we packed up our things, loaded them into Torstein's SUV, and drove with him, Axel, Raynor . . . and Bodil. Knowing the alignment was tonight—and that it was likely her only chance to actually see Sverrir before he made his play to destroy our world—she'd insisted on coming with us. Torstein had agreed. He'd keep her safely in his hotel room until the alignment began. What he hadn't told her was that his protections were weakening . . . and that the dark magic would take her soon.

I hoped she got the peace she needed.

Leaving the sorority house was bittersweet—whatever tonight's outcome, we wouldn't be coming back. If Sverrir was successful, our world would disappear . . . and we'd likely blip out of existence right along with it. But his failure depended on our fighting for our lives . . . and possibly losing them in the process. The best-case scenario was for us to fight, win, and live—a highly unlikely outcome that would result in our safe and swift return to Valkyris via magic dagger transport. In none of these scenarios could we return to the cheerful warmth of Kappa Mu.

I wasn't sure how I felt about that.

My fingertips grazed my bedspread as I took one last look around the blue and silver, snowflake-themed room that had been our home for the past few weeks. We may not have been the "Norwegian exchange students" our housemates believed us to be. But they'd welcomed us into their sisterhood and given us hope that someday, the brutish ways of the Viking tribes would be laid to rest. More societies like Valkyris really were possible, if only we had the strength and patience to build them.

I clung to that thought on our two-hour drive south.

"Do you want me to fix your pillow?" I asked Bodil quietly. The two of us sat on opposite sides of the back row of Torstein's SUV. Bodil's legs were stretched across the middle seat, and her back was propped against the window. Her skin was pale, and her eyes had dark circles. But she held herself with a regal grace —she had the air of a warrior determined to complete her mission.

"I can do it." She reached a shaky arm behind her and slowly nudged the pillow higher. She rested her head against it, a thin sweat coating her forehead.

I placed my hand on her arm. "Are you sure you want to do this? It can't be easy to see someone you used to love in, well . . . in the state he's in now."

"I know it doesn't make sense. And I realize there's likely no reaching him. But if there's any chance I can help you take him off this path . . ." Bodil smiled sadly. "Wouldn't you do anything to help Axel?"

"Of course," I said without hesitation.

Bodil glanced at the wavy, brown man-bun seated in front of us. "He's an honorable man, Ingrid. The two of you are good for one another."

"True," I said with a smile. "Though we definitely get on each other's last nerves."

"You challenge each other," Bodil corrected. "The best relationships do. I hope you never forget how special your bond is."

"I won't," I said quietly. "But I do worry."

"About?"

"I care for Axel a great deal." I bit down on my

bottom lip. "And our jobs are dangerous. We're in life-or-death situations almost daily on this mission, and gods only knows what the next one will bring—if we're lucky enough to live to see it. Some days it's hard to not let fear overwhelm me. I don't know how you survived for so long without Sverrir, but I don't think I could have done it if I were in your place. You're a stronger woman than I am."

"That's not true, and you know it." Bodil smiled softly. "You're every bit as strong as me. You consistently rise to any occasion that is thrust upon you. As you will continue to do."

"I don't know about that," I muttered.

"Well I do," Bodil said forcefully. "You're a true fighter, Ingrid. And so is Axel. You believe in what is good and honorable, and you share this light with the world. The two of you are perfectly suited to one another. Such a match is a rare blessing. And as such, the gods will endeavor to protect it. Besides, worrying never helped anyone. And it certainly never changed the course of events—not for the better, at any rate."

Bodil's words loosened the knot that had taken up permanent residence in my chest. In that moment, I knew I couldn't hold onto my fear any longer. Whatever the future held, I needed to enjoy every moment of the time Axel and I *did* have together. The arrogant, overprotective assassin owned my heart. He always had, and he always would—no matter how much he drove me crazy. Worrying wasn't going to change whatever might come. But it would destroy the time we did get to share. If I were to die tomorrow, I wanted to do so knowing I'd lived every moment with Axel to its fullest.

"Thanks Bodil." I tilted my head. "How do you already know us so well?"

Bodil's lips pressed together in a wry smile. "When you spend gods-only-knows how long trapped in a frozen wasteland, you learn to be perceptive."

I could only imagine.

Bodil coughed, the rasping sound rattling her chest. Axel turned around and held out a bottle of water. "Do you need a drink?"

"Thank—*cough, cough*—you." Bodil brought the bottle to her lips. When she'd finished, Axel took it from her trembling hands.

"Let me know when you need more," he said gently. Bodil nodded.

"See?" she murmured when he turned back around. "A good man."

"He's okay," I said with a wink.

Bodil reached over to rest her hand on my arm. "Just enjoy one another," she urged me. "You never know what the future holds."

It was true—especially so in our circumstance. Life back home was beautiful but unpredictable—fulfilling yet unsettled. We never knew what threats or joys might meet us each day, but we greeted every morning with hopeful hearts. We were lucky to be a part of such a progressive clan—to live on an island blessed by the gods and gifted with magic. But with those blessings came the responsibility of protecting our lifestyle . . . a challenge that would be put to the test tonight. If we failed to stop Sverrir, then we failed to save Valkyris. And if we failed to save our home . . . there was no telling what kind of world would be born from Sverrir's darkness.

When we reached the Hotel Del Coronado, I did a quick assessment of the massive structure. With its white walls, red roof, and whimsical design, the hotel was nothing short of spectacular. It was overwhelming from a strategic standpoint. The hotel had countless rooms, hallways, and outdoor nooks in which a dark mage could hide. But its beauty was undeniable. For the briefest of moments, I let myself appreciate the thoroughly modern monument.

Then I got straight to work.

Torstein dropped us at the front while he went around to park the car. I shouldered my bag, did my best to conceal my sheathed sword, and slipped my hand into Axel's.

"Well." I took a breath. "Here we are."

"Here we are," he said calmly. Then he nudged me with his shoulder. "It's all going to work out."

I appreciated him saying that. But despite our efforts, Sverrir had outwitted us so many times before . . .

"It is," Axel urged. "You've got to trust me on this, Shieldmaiden."

I stood on tiptoe and kissed his cheek. "Even with everything you've seen, you always manage to look on the bright side."

"Seems more enjoyable than the alternative." Axel winked.

My heart swelled. This man . . . this life . . . they were everything I'd never known I needed. And I had one more shot to hold onto them.

I squared my shoulders, turned to the hotel entrance, and squeezed Axel's hand. "Let's do this."

Despite the looming threat—or maybe because of it—I took my time getting ready for the formal. Janna, Brigga and I had borrowed dresses from Kenzi and Kayla. We joined the sisters in their suite, where they were primping with Meri. Tall stools stood by the window, while two women I didn't recognize twisted hair into intricate styles.

"Do you girls want your hair and makeup done?" Kayla asked as she ushered us through the door. "Tara's just finishing up on Meri, and Sarri should be done with Kenzi in a few."

Kenzi batted her long lashes. "I went for a major cat-eye."

"And I'm going full princess." Meri patted her elaborate updo. "It's one of my last formals, so I might as well go all out."

"Don't touch your hair!" the woman with the comb tutted.

Meri shot us a sheepish grin.

"I want my hair done just like Meri's," Brigga bubbled. "Only different."

Meri's hair helper nodded.

"I'll put your dresses in the closet." Kayla took the long bags from our arms and hung them up. Then she gestured to a snack-covered table. "Help yourself to anything that looks good. We take our party prep *very* seriously."

"I can see that," Janna said. "Is it always like this before your events?"

"Only the big ones," Meri said. "Formals, initiation, the usual."

Kayla bounded across the room. "What about you? Do the girls in the Oslo chapter go all out for dances?"

"All out," I lied. "We really get into, uh, preparations."

"Okay, Meri, you're done," Meri's stylist said from the window. "Go see what you think."

Meri stood and walked to the bathroom. A moment later, she emerged with a huge grin on her face. "I love it! Thank you, Tara."

"Of course." Tara turned to Brigga. "Are you ready?"

"Yes." Brigga skipped to the stool. "Now, I want Meri's updo—but only *half up*," she clarified. "With curls tumbling down my back, and a few wisps framing my face to draw out my cheekbones."

Janna arched one brow. "That is extremely specific."

Brigga shrugged. "I know what looks good on me."

Of course she did.

"Your turn, Ingrid." Kenzi stood. Her glossy, black hair was tucked up in a loose knot, and her already gorgeous eyes popped against the thick black lines drawn around her lashes.

"You look beautiful," I said as I took her place on the stool. "As you always do."

"I'm not usually big on makeup—you've seen me at yoga." She laughed. "But this is pretty fun."

Sarri ran her fingers through my mane. "These thick curls are *amazing.* You really have the whole Viking warrior vibe going for you."

She had no idea.

"Do you have something specific in mind?" Sarri asked.

"No. You can do whatever you want."

Sarri's eyes lit up. "Really?"

"Really."

"What color is your dress?" she asked.

"Green."

"Pale emerald," Kayla corrected.

Sarri nodded. "I have the perfect idea."

For the next half hour, she braided, pinned and tucked while I tried not to think about alignments, and dark mages, and the possible end of our world. She moved on to my makeup next, finally clapping her hands together and announcing, "Perfection!"

"Oh, Ingrid," Kayla trilled from across the room. "You look *beautiful*."

"You really do," Kenzi added. "Go. Check it out."

I walked to the bathroom and peered into the mirror. My breath caught as I took in the intricate crown of braids arching across my head, the mass of glossy curls cascading down my back, and the gold liner rimming my eyes. The green shadow that dusted my lids was a near perfect match to my dress. If I had to go into an end-of-world battle, this was *definitely* the way to look.

"You made me a warrior princess." I grinned as I returned to the suite. "I love it."

"I knew you would." Sarri waved at Janna. "Okay, last one. Come, come."

Janna took her seat while the rest of us slipped into our dresses. When we were ready, Kayla filled glass flutes with pink, bubbly liquid. "This calls for a toast. To a memorable evening."

Kenzi raised her glass. "To sisterhood. To the sisters we chose, and the ones that we didn't—but still love anyway."

Kayla stuck out her tongue. "Ha, ha."

Janna raised her flute. "To kindness. You all took us in and made us your family. We're lucky to know you."

"We're the lucky ones," Kayla said. "You've brought a lot of fun to Kappa Mu. I'm so glad you came into our lives!"

My heart tugged as I raised my own glass. "To new possibilities. We had no idea what we'd find when we walked into your sorority—and we have no idea what life will hold once we leave. But I wouldn't trade the adventures we've shared for anything."

I meant every word. I'd seen things over the past two months that would have been beyond comprehension back in Valkyris. But I was grateful for the moments I'd spent in study hours, exchanges, and at Monday night dinners. I'd experienced college life, learned the mysterious traffic cycles of the Los Angeles freeways, and discovered the joys—and pains—of yoga. And although I'd been fighting an unimaginable force of evil, my time with Kappa Mu had given me a lot of happiness.

I clinked my glass to my friends', and locked the moment into my memory. Then I put down my drink, followed Janna and Brigga back to our room, and got ready for the battle of my life.

"Whoa. Ingrid. You look . . ." Axel let out a low whistle. My cheeks warmed at the heat radiating from his hungry stare. His eyes smoldered, and his hands tensed, and he looked for all the world like the assassin that he was.

I was only too happy to be locked in his sights.

"You like the dress?" I spun a tight circle in the hallway outside the ballroom. We'd decided to meet downstairs to stash our weapons somewhere close to the event room. Easy access would be key in staving off a potential attack. But before we saved the world, my boyfriend needed to appreciate what I could look like when I *wasn't* in my work clothes.

Even if I never wore anything like this ever again.

"I like what's *in* the dress." His voice was gravelly. "Holy Helheim, Ingrid. You're a warrior goddess."

"I'm a warrior goddess every day. Nice of you to finally notice."

"You know what I mean." Axel's eyes moved slowly from the braids that gave way to wild curls, to the low neckline of my gown. He lingered there for a few moments longer than necessary before sweeping his gaze along my dress.

I twirled again and the hem flared with the movement, its filmy fabric fanning out around my ankles. The garment was surprisingly easy to move in. Its full, floor-length skirt was made of a gauzy fabric Kayla had called tulle. Thanks to an intricate series of gathers, it flowed dreamily in cloud-like puffs, forming an "*A*" that would make it considerably easier to front-kick in, should the need arise. Its top was fitted, with a plunging neckline and wide shoulder straps that gave way to a high back—perfect for concealing a magical, highly sought-after dagger. A thin strip of fabric was belted around my waist, tied in a low bow at the back. The dress was dreamy, and regal, and full of whimsy— definitely different from anything I'd ever worn before.

"You look *spectacularly* beautiful," Axel concluded. "I am one lucky man."

"You are," I agreed. Then I stood on tiptoe to kiss him. "But then, I'm pretty lucky, too."

"Darn right you are."

Raynor popped his head around the corner. "If you two are done admiring yourselves, I think I found a place to store our weapons."

Axel gave me one last, long look before extending his hand and lacing his fingers through mine. He palmed his broadsword in the other hand and pointed it at Raynor. "Lead the way."

"It's back here." Janna poked her head out of a door just off the ballroom. "It's a storage closet—extra tables and chairs from the look of it. I'm guessing they've already done their setup on all these rooms, so it should stay empty."

"Sounds good." I deposited my sword and shield but kept my fighting blade strapped to my thigh. Weapons may not have been allowed at modern-day dances, but a girl could never be too careful.

"Freia's dagger is still secure, *ja*?" Axel closed the door behind him, then slid his hand up my back. His fingers stilled when they brushed the metal.

"It's there." I moved toward the ballroom. "Right between my shoulder blades."

"Good. Now let's get to this party. We still have a few hours before midnight, and I intend to show my girl a good time."

I arched my brow. "Pretty confident in your dancing abilities, are you, Andersson?"

"Yes." He leaned down and whispered in my ear, "I meant what I said, Shieldmaiden. You look absolutely amazing tonight."

I tilted my head, studying his black suit and white bowtie. He'd left his hair down, so it fell in auburn waves around his neatly trimmed beard. *Mmm.*

He kissed my fingertips, then pulled me to him and snaked his arm around my back. He lowered his head, pressing his lips against mine and sending a surge of heat all the way to my toes. I reached up to wind my fingers through his hair. I tugged him closer, deepening the kiss and—

"You're blocking the door." Raynor cleared his throat.

"Huh? Oh. Right." I reluctantly stepped out of Axel's arms. "Raincheck?"

"You'd better believe it," he said. He laced his fingers through mine and tugged me toward the ballroom.

The moment I stepped inside I was assaulted by flashing lights, writhing bodies, and an incessant, rhythmic beat. Flower-covered tables surrounded a packed wooden floor, on which my ballgown-clad housemates danced like it was the last night of the world. All inhibitions had apparently been checked at the door. It was nothing like the refined balls we had back home, with our buttoned-up bunads, and stiff-backed dances. This event was wild, and carefree, and by all accounts, immeasurably *fun*.

I couldn't wait to jump in.

"There you are." Torstein's voice pulled my focus. The light mage sat at the table closest to the door, his normally free hair tied up in a loose man-bun. He wore the same black suit and white bowtie as Axel and Raynor, but instead of a relaxed grin, his lips were set in a tight grimace. "I've confirmed the exact location of the convergence. The planets should channel their energy about half a mile from here. It's going to take place on a beach."

"Of course it is." Raynor frowned. "Because nothing's easier than fighting in sand."

"It's softer to fall in," I pointed out.

"That's my girl." Axel pulled me close. "Ever the optimist."

"The location means that Sverrir will *definitely* be nearby—if he's not already in place, he will be soon." Torstein pulled two faintly glowing crystals from his pocket. "I'm going to scan the hotel perimeter. If he's in the vicinity, he may have picked up on the resonance of *these* and come to collect. A full set's bound to be stronger than a partial."

"I thought one was still missing," Brigga said.

"He got that one too." Torstein's voice was void of emotion. "Earlier tonight."

"How do you—"

"Don't ask." Torstein frowned. "Just tell me who's up for running perimeter with me."

"I'll do it," I offered.

"No." Torstein and Axel spoke at the same time.

"He still needs the dagger," Torstein reminded me. "We don't want you anywhere near him."

"I'm part of this team," I pointed out. "It's not like I'm going to sit out the fight."

Axel shifted uncomfortably.

Torstein stared him down. "You didn't tell her?"

"Didn't tell me what?" I set my hand on my hip.

"Raynor, Brigga, run the perimeter with me." Torstein eyed Axel. "Janna, Brigga, you protect Ingrid."

"Since when have I ever needed protecting?" I challenged.

Torstein met my gaze. "Since that dagger in your possession became the only object capable of saving the world from total annihilation."

A lump lodged in my throat. "*Ja*. Well . . ."

"Tell her, Axel. I have to go." With that, Torstein rose from the table and swept out of the room. Brigga and Raynor followed.

"Tell me what?" I turned to Axel.

"It's too loud in here. I'll tell you out there." He jutted his head to the door. "Come on."

"I'm coming with you." Janna laced her arm through mine. "And for the record, Ingrid does *not* need protecting. No matter what she has in her possession."

"I know that." Axel held open the door. The three of us walked into the hallway, moving slowly toward the hotel gift shop. "But Torstein is worried. He's seen what Sverrir is capable of."

"Has he seen what I'm capable of?" I growled.

"Hey." Axel reached out to touch my elbow. "I'm on

your team. If you want to fight, then you fight. I certainly have no intention of telling you what to do. Not now, not ever."

"Smart assassin," I said.

"But Torstein does have a point."

Janna and I treated Axel to matching glares.

"Not about you needing to be looked after—that's just dumb." He frowned. "But about the dagger being a liability."

"I won't lose it, Axel."

"I'm not worried about you letting it off your person. I'm worried because I know you'll fight to the death to keep it safe. And I'm not exactly thrilled about the idea of losing *you*."

My jaw unclenched. "Axel . . ."

"Hear me out." Pain danced across his features. "What if—*if*—you and I didn't go to the convergence site at midnight. Or you and Janna, if you think she's a better protector. Sverrir has to know you'll show up on the beach. He knows we'll try to take him down, so he's expecting the dagger to come to him. But if you stay behind, he won't have everything he needs to do his spell. He'll be one magic blade short, waiting for a prize that never comes. He can't destroy the world if he doesn't have all the tools."

"And you think that a portion of our team will be able to do what we failed to accomplish as a whole?" I asked. "We've gone head-to-head with Sverrir fully manned. There's no chance we can take him down if two of our members sit this one out."

"I just—" Axel's voice cracked. "I don't want to lose you. And I know you'll do whatever it takes to fight for Valkyris."

"True. But I have no intention of dying tonight."

"Ingrid, I—"

"Listen." I unlinked my arm from Janna's. "I get where you're coming from. Believe me, I do. But if I sit this out—if Sverrir doesn't get the dagger tonight—then he's just going to keep coming for it. Maybe in this century, maybe in another. He's *never* going to give up."

"Ingrid has a point," Janna said quietly.

"If we don't capture him tonight, Valkyris will never be safe. We'll always be looking over our shoulder, waiting for him to show up and steal Freia's dagger." I wrung my fingertips together. "Or worse, we'll just fade from existence because he's stolen it in another timeline—and we never even saw it coming."

Axel rubbed his jaw. "I just wish there was another way."

"I do too," I admitted. "But there's not. We have to finish this. Tonight."

Axel's shoulders drooped. He reached out and took my hand. "Good thing you had the best trainer in Valkyris."

"*Ja.*" I blinked. "Janna did a *great* job teaching me."

"I did," Janna agreed.

"Ha. Ha." Axel rolled his eyes.

We stopped outside of the gift shop. As we turned

back toward the ballroom, an angry girl shouted from the store.

"Stop it! Stop throwing things at me!"

I cringed. "I know that voice."

"I said *stop it*! Wherever you are, just cut it out!"

Janna peered into the store window. "What is Lexi upset about?"

"No idea." I moved in beside her to find Lexi standing next to a row of candy, stamping her sequin-heeled foot. "But she looks *really* mad."

"When doesn't she look mad?" Janna crossed her arms.

I snorted.

Lexi's head whipped around. When she spotted me, her lips curled up in a sneer. "*You.*"

"Uh-oh," I muttered.

Lexi stormed out of the store. She stopped in front of me with her hands balled into tight fists. "I don't know how you did it, but you'd better knock it off right now."

"Knock what off?" I asked.

"Stop throwing things at me." Lexi's shoulders trembled.

"I was out here," I pointed out. "Behind this massive glass window. How could I possibly have been throwing anything at you?"

"I *said* I don't know how you're doing it," Lexi snapped. "Maybe you have some kind of wire set up. Or you paid off one of the workers to stand behind the shelf and push books off of it."

"Hold on." Axel held up his hands. "You're saying somebody is throwing *books* at you?"

"Yes." Lexi rubbed her forehead. "Big books, too. They hurt."

I bit back my laugh.

"It isn't funny, *Inga*."

"It's still Ingrid," I said calmly. "And I can assure you, I had no part in your book assault."

"You should be more careful who you tick off. The hotel *is* haunted." Morgan stepped out of the gift shop holding a small bag. "Guests have reported incidents like this before. You ought to let the concierge know—I'm sure he'd love to document it."

"It wasn't a *ghost*, Morgan." Lexi crossed her arms and shifted her weight onto her back foot. "It was Ingrid. She's had it in for me ever since she got here. And I have *had it*."

She turned on one high heel and stormed toward the ballroom. She spun back around, slammed her hands onto her hips, and yelled at me. "Don't think you'll get away with this. I'm going to—"

Her tirade muted as my brain sounded a warning signal. A small, black circle had just appeared behind Lexi. It swirled and sparked in a pattern I knew all too well. In the time it took me to kick off my heels and sprint down the hall, it had expanded to the size of a door.

"Lexi! Get down!"

"Ingrid's *attacking* me!" Lexi shrieked. "Help!"

I threw myself on top of her. My shoulder slammed

195

into her chest as I wrenched us away from the rapidly growing portal. We landed in a heap, Lexi's pointed nails clawing violently at my back.

"You want a fight? I'll give you the fight of your—"

I covered her mouth with one hand. "Shut *up*, Lexi. You are in danger. Very, very big danger. If you have any idea what's good for you, you will run away from that portal *and do not look back.*"

Lexi bit my palm. I rolled away from her and swore.

"What *portal?*" Lexi spat. "What are you talking about?"

I pointed to the massive, black vortex filling the corridor behind her. "That one."

Lexi's face paled. "Oh my God."

"*Something very evil* is about to walk out of it. So get the Helheim out of here," I warned. "Now."

Lexi didn't say another word. She scrambled to her feet, and took off running. Axel and Janna raced to my side.

"Stay clear of that thing," Axel cautioned.

I glanced down the hallway. Morgan hadn't moved from her spot in front of the gift shop. She held one hand over her mouth, her other arm in the air. If her face wasn't wracked with terror, I'd have thought she was in class, about to ask a question.

"Morgan, you too," I warned. "Get out of here."

"What's going on?" Morgan's voice shook.

My eyes sought out Axel's. How much could we tell her without upending her entire notion of reality?

"Remember all of those things we learned in Folklore?" Axel asked calmly. "About mages, and fountains of youth, and enchanted stones?"

"Ye-ee-eesss." Morgan's teeth chattered.

"Well, they're true. All of them." Axel eyed the sparking portal. "Now *run*."

"I'll get the weapons from storage." Janna sprinted down the hallway. "Don't engage until I'm back."

Morgan stared at me. "Do you need help?"

"Help us by making sure everybody stays out of this hallway except Torstein, Brigga and Raynor," I pleaded. "And tell Kenzi and Kayla and everyone else thank you. For everything."

Morgan blinked. "You sound like you're saying goodbye."

My throat tightened. *I am.* But I held Morgan's gaze and said firmly, "Thank you, Morgan. You've been a true friend to us. We wouldn't have made it this far without you."

"Ingrid . . ."

"Run, Morgan," I said as the portal sparked again.

Morgan nodded. She sprinted toward us and threw her arms around me. "I'm going to miss you. Wherever you're going."

I squeezed her back. "We'll miss you too. Now, go!"

She shot me one last smile before skirting around the portal and racing for the ballroom. When she'd rounded the corner, I turned my attention to the thick, black hole.

"It's nearly open, and we are seriously lacking in

weapons. Where's Janna?" I lifted my skirt and drew my fighting dagger.

Axel dropped into a battle stance. He pulled his own dagger from his ankle just as pale hands reached around either edge of the portal. They pulled the sides apart, expanding the blackness until it was wide enough to fit a body. A boot stepped from the hole, followed by a leg, a cloak, and the jowly face of the one being in all the world I least wanted to see. Sverrir had arrived.

And he looked ready to kill.

## CHAPTER 14

"**WE HAVE TO DRAW** him out of the hotel."
Axel stepped carefully backward. "We don't
want any civilian casualties."

"Got any suggestions?" I tightened my grip on my
dagger.

"*Ja.*" Janna charged down the hallway, her arms
loaded with weapons. "Run like Helheim!"

She flung her arms out, sliding swords and shields
across the ground. I bent to snatch mine up, then
turned and sprinted for the exit. The air crackled
behind me, but I didn't look to see if it came from the
portal or from Sverrir. The dark mage wouldn't think
twice about lighting up that ballroom—not if it might
make me give up the dagger. We had to get him as far
from the hotel as possible, so he didn't have any lever-
age. And the fastest way to do that was . . .

"Axel," I shouted over my shoulder as I thundered
into the lobby. "Call for Rufus!"

"What?" His footsteps pounded right behind me.

"Call Rufus! We need a ride!"

"On it." Axel came up beside me. He muttered into his bracelet, then charged past the main desk. As he neared the glass entry, he waved his blade and barreled past several surprised guests—all of whom jumped hurriedly from his path. When he reached the mat, he spun around and held up his sword. "I'll hold him off. You just get on Rufus when he shows."

"No way. I'm not leaving you alone with—"

"Sverrir will follow Freia's dagger," Janna shouted. "If he's focused on you, he's not going to kill as many bystanders."

My heart seized. Letting Axel risk his life for me went against every fiber of my being. But I knew what I had to do. And I had to believe that Axel wouldn't let me down—not now, not *ever*.

"Right." I pumped my legs and lowered my head. "Just keep that door open."

I charged past the uniformed doorman and leapt down the red-carpeted steps. When I reached the pavement, I hung a sharp right and ran. Footsteps from behind let me know I wasn't alone, but I could only hope it was Janna on my heels. Because if Sverrir was this close already, the fight was over before it had even begun.

"Ingrid! The dragon is coming!" Janna's voice sent a whoosh of breath from my chest.

*Thank gods.*

"Where is he?" I didn't slow down as I scanned the sky.

"There!" Janna pointed toward the beach. Rufus swooped low overhead, likely searching the coastline for his owner. I altered my course and ran for the lizard.

"Rufus!" I waved my sword, hoping the moonlight would catch on the metal. "Rufus, down here!"

The dragon landed on the sand. His long neck snaked from side to side.

"He can't find us. Come on." I ran faster, closing the distance between us and our ride.

Janna passed me just before we reached the beach. She banged her sword on her shield as she kicked off her shoes and ran toward the water. "Rufus! Help!"

The dragon turned his head. Something akin to recognition flickered across his eyes—though it could just as easily have been that creepy third eyelid. He bounded across the sand, surprising a handful of late-night beachgoers. They ran screaming for the hotel, no doubt convinced they were about to die.

Considering what was happening behind me, they may not have been off-base.

"Rufus—we need you to take us to Axel. Drop down so we can climb your leg!" I didn't even flinch at issuing commands to an enchanted iguana-dragon. Nor was I surprised when the animal did what I asked. Rufus bent his knees and lowered his head. I grabbed his spikes and pulled myself onto his thigh. My foot slipped and I flung my arms around his neck, scrambling as I struggled to climb higher. Rufus swung his neck around, nipped lightly at the back of my dress, and lifted me onto his back like a mother cat guiding her kitten. His dragon breath was hot on my bare shoulders, but thank the gods he did not flame. Instead, he lowered his head again, took Janna's gown between his pointed teeth, and lifted her into place behind me.

"Thank you," I called to the dragon.

He snorted a puff of thick, white smoke.

"Axel's over there." I pointed to the hotel. "Go get him!"

Rufus pushed himself to his feet and pounded across the sand. In ten short steps, he'd spread his wings and launched into the air. I flattened myself against his back and held on for dear life. Behind me, Janna's nails dug into my waist. Neither of us were particularly happy fliers, but we were professional enough to keep our mouths firmly shut.

Rufus dove. I clung desperately to his scales. Air whooshed from my chest as we landed in the grass beside the hotel. Seconds later, Axel slid into place in front of me. I sat up, and transferred my clinging arms from the dragon to his back.

"Torstein, Brigga, and Raynor are heading to the beach," Axel said. "I saw them when I came outside."

"And Sverrir?" I asked.

"He's close." Axel grimaced. "Rufus, head for the water!"

The dragon ran a few steps before jumping in the

air. Wind chilled my bare arms as he climbed, flying high above the pointed red rooftops of the hotel.

"Dive," Axel commanded.

I gripped my boyfriend's back as Rufus launched himself down. My stomach lurched but I swallowed hard. *Please, gods, don't let me be sick. Not on top of Axel.*

"Torstein!" Axel shouted. "Head north!"

I peeled my eyelids open and peered down. Torstein saluted from the sand. He waved Raynor and Brigga forward, and darted up the beach.

"What's our plan?" I called to Axel.

"We still want him clear of the hotel," Axel yelled back. "But we also want to draw him away from the convergence site. If we can keep him off-course, maybe the energy won't come close enough to—"

"Look out!" Janna screamed in my ear. A red beam shot up from the ground, narrowly missing Rufus' wing. The dragon angled sharply to the left.

"Hold on tight!" Axel shouted.

He shifted his weight. Rufus dropped into what felt like a death dive.

"Axel!" I shrieked.

"Rufus, flame!" Axel yelled.

Heat slammed into my face as the dragon released a massive burst of fire. It charred the sand, leaving fiery embers in its wake. I could only assume Sverrir had been the target.

"Did we hit him?" I asked.

"No. He ported out."

"What?" I whipped my head around. "Where did he go?"

A spark of light flashed on the sand. Sverrir appeared a short distance up the beach. An array of objects surrounded his feet.

"Never mind—there he is." I pointed. "He must have collected some things on his port because he—oh. Oh, no."

"He's got the ingredients?" Janna guessed.

"It sure as Helheim looks like it." Axel leaned forward. "But the convergence site is south of here. And it's not supposed to happen for another hour. Why would he bring them here unless . . ."

"Unless the calculations were wrong." I blinked at the sky. A row of bright dots twinkled in a nearly straight line. "Oh my gods, it's happening. It's happening *right now.*"

"We have to attack," Janna said.

"He doesn't have the dagger," Axel countered. "If we keep Ingrid airborne—"

"We have to take him out." I stared at the ground. "He'll never stop coming for us. But if we capture him now, he won't be able to hurt us—in the future, or the past, or ever."

"We'd better do it fast," Janna warned. "Those planets look awfully close."

"Good thing I'm a fast flier." Axel lowered his head. He issued his command, and Rufus soared up the beach. The dragon dropped low, his toes skimming the ocean and sending a spray of saltwater splashing against my bare feet. The tulle of my skirt clung to my legs, and I squeezed my knees against the dragon's ribs to keep from slipping.

We'd nearly reached Sverrir when a bright flash erupted in the sky.

"It's starting!" Torstein's voice boomed from the beach. He, Brigga, and Raynor were nearly even with us—the light mage must have ported them in. He'd also brought Bodil, who floated in some kind of suspended bubble. Now, my friends ran—and hovered—parallel to our flight path. They narrowed the distance between themselves and Sverrir with impressive speed. Raynor carried his sword—he must have grabbed it from the storage closet when he'd left with Torstein. And the light mage had fired up a white orb. He tossed it between his palms while keeping an eye on the sky. I followed his sightline to the spot where the planets had very nearly come together.

*Oh, gods. Are we too late?*

The white beam came from the farthest of the twinkling lights. It shot forward, illuminating each planet in turn until they formed a single, interconnected string. In the time it took me to send up a silent prayer, the beam burst down from the sky. It hit the ocean with a deafening *boom*. A massive wave erupted at the impact site. It moved swiftly toward the shore, the glowing, glittering mass of water driving straight for the spot where Sverrir stood.

"Stop him!" I screamed. "Before it hits!"

"Rufus!" Axel ordered. "Get there!"

The dragon lowered his head and flapped harder. Icy wind whipped against my wet legs. Hope flickered in my heart as I held tight to Axel's waist. This was a race against nature—one we could win. The wave had momentum, but we had motivation. We were *going* to capture Sverrir. I firmly believed it—with every last fiber of my heart.

Until the moment that we didn't.

## CHAPTER 15

THE WAVE CRASHED AGAINST the shore at the exact moment that we did. Rufus' feet slammed into the ground, launching Janna and I off his back. I tucked my knees to my chest as I soared through the air. The second my bare feet hit the sand, I drew my sword and charged at Sverrir. Janna's battle cry sounded behind me. The thunder of footsteps let me know that Torstein, Brigga, Raynor and the still-suspended Bodil weren't far behind. It was seven on one, and we had a dragon on our side. Victory was all but assured.

*Snap!*

The sound echoed across the beach. Its deep vibration resonated against the front of my skull, as if it were trying to push its way out. The world spun, and the edges of my vision grew blurry. Heat built between my shoulder blades, low at first, then building to the point of pain. I transferred my sword to one hand and reached overhead to claw at what I assumed was the source of the inferno—Freia's dagger. But my fingertips jammed into hard wood. I'd forgotten my shield was still on my back. The heat beneath it intensified, and I wrenched my arm to my waist to try and snake it up the back of my shirt. My fingers wrapped around the dagger, and I wedged them beneath the straps holding it down. The metal blade sparked, sending a surge of heat through my hand. I gritted my teeth and tried again. This time, I managed to wrap my palm around the handle.

And then everything went black.

For a seeming eternity, I spiraled in an endless void of darkness. The moment before, my senses had been completely overwhelmed. Icy seawater had weighed down my skirt while burning metal seared my back. The flash of lights had lit my vision—both from the crashing wave and the beams thrown between Sverrir and Torstein. And the shouts of my teammates had filled the empty beach, their cries signaling the conclusion of something inevitable and irreversible. But now, there was nothing. No sound. No sensation. No sign of life. The entire world was cloaked in darkness.

My stomach dropped. *Did we lose?*

A burst of light turned everything white. It came from above—a single stream illuminating what looked to be a long, vertical shaft. Its walls shimmered slightly, as if it were made of pearl—or the extremely fancy plates we'd used for formal meals at Kappa Mu. I continued to fall, but I was no longer alone. Now,

Janna tumbled beside me. Her intricate updo had come undone, so her wild, black braids whipped against her face. She'd managed to remove her shield, and she held it in front of her chest as she spiraled. Brigga and Raynor were directly across from me, and Bodil was just above—still suspended in her bubble. Axel was slightly below us, atop a flailing Rufus. The dragon's wings flapped frantically but they didn't seem to be doing him any good. Rufus and Axel fell as fast as the rest of us. We spiraled downward in a descent that was sure to kill us—if we weren't dead already. Maybe this was the path to Valhalla. Or maybe I'd been hit on the head and was smack in the middle of an epic hallucination. Or maybe—

*Snap!*

My body was wrenched upward, the sudden motion shooting jolts of pain through my joints. Now I was traveling up . . . but instead of falling, I was being jerked by my limbs. Sharp jabs fired through my elbows, shoulders, knees and hips until I thought I might be ripped apart. I squeezed my eyes shut and willed the agony to end.

A few seconds later, it did. My upward trajectory stopped along with it. Now I was moving . . . nowhere?

I pulled my shield from my back, and cautiously pried my eyes open. All around me, my friends were suspended in the air. They seemed to float, their bodies hovering around the moonlit shaft in a bizarre state of suspension. Below, Rufus continued flapping his wings. But now, the motion carried Axel up to our level.

"What the Helheim is going on?" Axel demanded.

"I have no idea." I drew my shoulders back, eliciting a fresh wave of pain. The skin beneath Freia's dagger felt as if it had spent the last few minutes inside a bonfire. It was tender, and probably badly blistered, but at least the agony was beginning to ebb.

*Is that because the dagger is gone?*

"Oh, gods. No." I turned my head, desperate to see if I'd lost our prize. I would never forgive myself if—

"Freia's dagger is still there," Brigga called from across the circle. "It looks like it burned a hole in your dress, but it's still strapped to you. I can see the blade."

"Thank gods." My torso slumped in relief. The motion stretched the charred skin, and I winced again. *Ouch.*

"But we didn't activate Freia's dagger," Janna pointed out. "So how are we in this . . . what exactly are we—"

Another flash interrupted my captain. I looked up— carefully, so as not to hurt my back again—to find Torstein barreling down the shaft. He fell back-first, his arms above his chest and his hands sending long, white beams up the cylinder. A second figure appeared above him—this one cloaked, and firing off shots of his own. I raised my shield as the two mages neared, and angled my sword so I could strike Sverrir on his descent.

He'd nearly reached me when he and Torstein slammed into an invisible wall. They lay in the center of the void, just out of my reach and frozen in a moment of suspended animation.

And then all Helheim broke loose.

The two mages dropped so they were on our level. Sverrir fired the first shot. The red beam burst from his hand and struck the wall behind me. Its surface crackled, then lit up in a brilliant flame. I leapt to the side, running for Janna before I realized *I was walking on air.* With nothing beneath my feet, I should have fallen straight down the shaft. But wherever we were, the laws of physics had ceased to apply.

*Don't think about it, Ingrid. Just fight.*

"Wait!" Bodil's rasp filled the void. We all froze as she floated lower. Torstein raised his hand, using whatever invisible force he possessed to keep her from getting too close to Sverrir.

"He's dangerous," Torstein warned.

"I don't—*cough, cough*—care." Bodil was even paler than I'd remembered. Her hands trembled, and her voice shook, but she held Torstein's gaze with a steady eye—and the determination of a chieftess. She'd sworn to use the last of her strength to try to stop Sverrir; to salvage at least some small part of the man she'd known.

But the dark mage was too far gone.

"Sver—*cough.* Sverrir," Bodil croaked. "Please, don't do this. You're—*cough*—more than—*cough*—a killer."

"You're dying," Sverrir spat. "This is the only way I can save you."

"You're—*cough*—better than this." A sheen broke out

across Bodil's forehead. She held out a hand, supporting her weight against the edge of her bubble. "Be the man I know you are—*cough*. Do it . . . *gasp* . . . for me . . ." Bodil rested the back of her head against the filmy surface that supported her.

Below, Sverrir ignited a fresh orb between his hands.

"On guard," Axel ordered. We all raised our weapons.

"I am doing this for you." Sverrir's voice cracked. "Everything I've done since you were taken from me was to find my way back to you."

"No." Bodil stared at him sadly. "This isn't who you are. I know you've—*cough*. Seen loss. I know—*cough, cough*—you're in pain. But you had to know I wouldn't want this for you. I only ever—*cough*—wanted you to be happy."

"I will be," Sverrir growled. "Once I reset the—"

Bodil broke into a coughing fit so fierce, Sverrir dropped his orb. She clutched at her chest and slumped against the wall of her bubble. As she drew a shaky breath, her eyes widened and she reached out to Sverrir. "Please," she rasped. "I—*cough*—lo—*cough, cough*." She slumped over. As she drew her final breath, her voice was no more than a whisper. "I love you."

And just like that, Bodil was gone.

Sverrir's rage was instant. He threw his head back and screamed into the void, then fired a series of orbs at my team. One nearly nicked my shoulder, and I hurriedly dropped into position. I lunged forward. My sword struck the dark mage's arm. He whirled around and fired another beam at me. My shield blocked his shot. Smoking wood filled the air, and I slammed my fist against my shield to stamp out the flame. Sverrir shook off his injury. He extended his arms to his sides, spun in a slow circle, and fired a fresh round. Flashes of red pinged off the walls, the seemingly endless column lighting up with bursts of crimson. My teammates went on the defense. Brigga and Raynor flung themselves onto the invisible ground. Axel drove Rufus farther down the tunnel. Torstein dusted the smoldering debris from his suit coat. And Janna and I jumped out of the path of neighboring shots. We crashed into each other, our swords reverberating with the contact. My shoulder slammed into the wall, and I landed hard on my back. Janna landed on top of me, sending the air whooshing from my lungs. I struggled to draw a breath. My captain rolled onto her knees, extended her hand, and helped me to stand.

"Get up, Ingrid. We don't want to give him any opportunity to—no!" Janna raised her sword. It deflected another blast. I raised my own weapon and dropped into a fighting stance, ready to cover my friend.

*Not today, Sverrir.*

As I prepared myself to attack, Torstein threw a white orb. It hit the dark mage's chest, and Sverrir doubled over. Raynor swung his sword low, slicing Sverrir across the ankle and drawing first blood. A low growl erupted from Sverrir's throat. He threw his arm out to the side, firing a red beam that whizzed past Brigga's face. She dropped to her knees, and flung herself forward.

"Augh!" Brigga rammed her dagger into Sverrir's calf. Raynor pulled her back just as the dark mage fired again. His beam pierced the air where Brigga's head had been, pinging off the wall and turning in a downward trajectory that sent it on a path straight to—

"Axel!" I screamed. "Look out!"

Axel shouted a command. Rufus swung his neck to one side and dove. The pair spiraled down, pulling away from the red beam then rotating upward. Rufus' wings flapped hard, carrying him back up the shaft until he and Axel were nearly level with the rest of us.

Axel shouted again, and Rufus shot a narrow stream of fire. It struck Sverrir from below, lighting up his cloak and forcing him to abandon his attack. With Sverrir distracted—and about to be engulfed in flames—I shuffled across the air and delivered a fierce front-kick. The dark mage stumbled back. He tripped on his own cloak. When he landed on his butt I kicked again—this time, a low roundhouse that landed square on his face with a satisfying *crack*. The blow vibrated from the top of my foot up my leg.

I'd struck gold.

Sverrir hissed. He brought his hands to his face, swiping away the blood that oozed from his nose. Janna delivered her own roundhouse, and the dark mage lashed out again. But he swiped at his eyes, and when he fired at me his aim was off. His shot missed, the beams leaning slightly to my left. They hit an already compromised section of the wall. A chunk tumbled down the shaft, but I kept my focus on the dark mage directly in front of me. He snaked one foot, hooking his boot around my ankle and nearly taking me down. Janna threw out her arm, and I grabbed onto it to steady myself. Then, I slammed my heel into Sverrir's ribcage. He swore loudly before rolling onto one side. His palms hit the unseen ground, and he pushed himself slowly up. If he stood, and if he got a clear shot at any one of us . . .

"No!" Torstein bellowed. He launched a massive orb —the biggest I'd seen him make—straight at the dark mage. Silver streaks lined the white sphere, so it sparked from within as it barreled through the air. Sverrir lifted a hand, probably intending to deflect it, but he lacked his usual strength. His fingertips shook and his arm dropped to his side.

The orb never wavered from its path.

The ball hit Sverrir in the chest, sparking silver streaks piercing its edges before circling the dark mage's body. He was immediately engulfed in what looked to be a tangle of unwieldy silver ropes. They wound together, tightening in a tapestry of impenetrable fibers. Magic sparked from within, lifting Sverrir in the air and lighting him up with blinding charges. His agony set my teeth on edge, but he'd left us no choice. If Torstein let up, the dark mage would seize the opportunity to gain the upper hand. We *had* to stop him from destroying our world. My team was the final line of defense—the silent shield protecting Valkyris, Los Angeles, and everything in between from the darkness this monster could cultivate. Sverrir's fall was inevitable. And yet . . .

An unexpected sadness flickered through me as the mage's screams fell silent. Despite Bodil's faith, Sverrir had proven himself unredeemable. There had been no doubt that the world he desired would be filled with immeasurable pain. But even so, I pitied him for the life he'd chosen. He could have—and should have—amounted to so much more. He'd just never been able to pull himself out of his own darkness.

He hadn't been as lucky as I was.

My eyes sought out Axel. The assassin kept Rufus just below the tightly bound mage. He watched as Sverrir's ropes loosened, and his torso folded over. "Is he . . ."

"Dead," Torstein confirmed. "He won't hurt anyone anymore."

My own chest caved in relief. "You're sure?"

"Yes." Torstein bent his fingers. The ropes guided Sverrir's limp body forward, so he rested beside Bodil. Torstein waved his hand, and the ropes settled on the ground. They unwound themselves, revealing an immobilized dark mage.

It was finally over.

I surveilled my team. Brigga clutched her arm. Raynor limped toward her, one of his pants legs singed at the knee. Torstein's chest rose and fell in a rare display of exhaustion. Janna leaned heavily on my arm, an ugly, green bruise already forming atop her bloodied shoulder.

And just below us, Axel slumped over his dragon. Exhaustion painted his stoic features as he tilted his head, met my eyes, and winked. "Nice work, Shieldmaiden."

"Back at you, assassi—augh!" The space between my shoulder blades burned anew. Freia's dagger dug into my skin, searing my flesh and driving me to my knees.

"Ingrid!" Axel called out. "Hold on. I'll—"

His words disappeared as we were sucked back into the darkness. The moonlight extinguished, the shaft disappeared, and I was once again enveloped in a silent void. The moment the world went black, the pain in my back dissolved. I reached behind me and gripped the hilt of Freia's dagger. It pulsed against my palm.

*That's new.*

A blinding light forced my eyes shut. Wind whipped against my face as I once again tumbled—gods only knew how far—before landing hard on my back. The impact sent the air whooshing from my chest. I opened my eyes, struggling for breath as I took in the heather-covered hillside, breathed in the salty, sea air, and in the distance, saw a beautifully familiar castle.

*Valkyris!*

"We're home!" Brigga's jubilant bleat came from my right.

"Thank gods!" Janna exhaled.

"It's about bloody time," Raynor muttered.

"My butt hurts." Axel rubbed his backside.

I turned my head. "You landed on Rufus' tail spike. Didn't you?"

The assassin carefully lifted his leg. "*Ja.* But I'd do it all again to be exactly where I am right now. Home. In Valkyris. On the North Sea—*not* the Pacific one. In a glorious field of wildflowers—not pavement and—"

"So *this* is Valkyris." Torstein's awed voice interrupted Axel's celebration. The light mage stood in the heather, his eyes wide as he turned in a slow circle. His gaze swept from the ocean to the castle to the *Dragehus.* As he took in the dragon's barn, his lips formed a small O. "In all my years, I've never seen anything like it."

"It's just home," I offered. Glorious, beautiful, exquisitely perfect *home.*

"Yes, but . . ." Torstein exhaled. "You have multiple dragons. They're magnificent."

Axel turned to the *Dragehus.* A trio of dragons roamed the pasture outside the large structure. A smaller, fourth dragon galloped happily nearby. He flapped his wings, lifted slightly off the ground, then fell face-first onto the grass.

"Killsvar is already learning to fly?" Axel shook his head. "How long were we gone?"

"Just under two months." A lyrical voice filled the meadow. "Thank the gods you're safely home!"

"Mother!" Raynor jumped to his feet. He ran between me and Janna, his feet flattening the heather as he made his way toward Chieftess Freia. She walked gracefully across the hill, her white-and-navy robes blowing in the light breeze. When she met

Raynor, she extended her arms and wrapped him in a warm hug.

"I'm so glad you're back," she said happily.

"Welcome home." Chief Halvar jogged over the knoll. When he reached Raynor, he patted him on the shoulder. "How was your journey?"

"Bizarre," Raynor said. "But successful. The target has been acquired."

Freia and Halvar scanned the hillside. Their eyes fell on the fallen dark mage and his long-ago love before sliding to Torstein. And then over to Rufus.

"It appears you have brought home a guest," Halvar said cautiously. "Or two."

"My new dragon's named Rufus. And this is Torstein." Axel stepped forward, still rubbing his injured backside. "He helped us complete our mission."

"I see." Freia pursed her lips. "And is he . . .?"

"He's a light mage from the future," Axel offered. "Though there, he'd been alive for centuries, so . . . maybe also the present?" The assassin rubbed his temples. "I can't wrap my head around time travel."

"Welcome, Torstein." Freia smiled at the still gaping mage. "It's an honor to have you on our island."

"It's an honor to be here," Torstein said reverently. "Valkyris is . . . it's . . ."

"You must be quite overwhelmed," Freia said kindly. "Why don't we take you all back to the castle? I'm sure you'd like to get cleaned up. I'll have the kitchen send up a nice meal for us to enjoy before we debrief."

"That sounds wonderful, Chieftess." Janna gestured

to the bodies. "But what should we do with the deceased?"

Halvar stepped closer to Sverrir. "Is this the dark mage that caused all the trouble?"

"It is," I confirmed.

"And the woman?"

"She was his love," Brigga said softly. "Though she never shared his darkness."

"I see. Well done, all of you." Halvar bowed his head. "May their spirits rest in peace."

Freia folded her hands together. After a moment of silence, she addressed her husband, "Halvar, please summon four of our warriors to keep watch over the bodies. We'll perform a proper funeral at sunset. The rest of you, follow me back to the castle. I'm sure you're quite exhausted from your journey."

Freia smiled beatifically and walked toward the castle. When my teammates followed, I turned to Axel.

"What are you going to do with Rufus?" I asked.

"Introduce him to the family, of course." Axel grinned at the pasture. The baby dragon jumped again. This time, he stayed in the air for a full four seconds. "Want to hang back with me?"

"There's nowhere I'd rather be."

"Freia," Axel called. "Ingrid and I are going to take care of the new dragon. We'll catch up with you."

"Of course." Freia nodded.

"Oh! I should probably give you this." I dropped my weapons and reached around my back. I unhooked

Freia's dagger and walked it to her side. "Thank you for entrusting it to me."

Freia took it from my palms. "It's warm."

"It got, uh, activated when the alignment tidal wave hit the beach."

Freia tilted her head, confusion coloring her delicate features.

"We'll explain at the castle," Axel offered. "Once we get Rufus settled in."

"Please don't rush." Freia smiled gently. "We have all the time in the world."

We did now. *Thank gods.*

I crossed to Axel's side and slipped my hand in his. Together, we led the iguana-dragon to the pasture where his new roommates apprised him cautiously. Axel made the introductions, then ducked into the *Dragehus* and returned with pouchfuls of raw meat and vegetables. He offered the dragons the treats, speaking calmly and drawing them together until they ate side by side. When the creatures were fully focused on their shared meal, Axel slung his arm around my shoulders and stared at the field.

"I have to be honest. I wasn't entirely sure I'd see this place again," he said.

"Me neither," I admitted.

"But here we are," Axel said easily. "See? I was right. As usual."

I rolled my eyes. "About what, exactly?"

"I told you, everything always works out. You worry way too much, Shieldmaiden."

"Maybe," I admitted. "I suppose we're a good balance that way. You trust that everything will work out. And I do the hard work and planning to ensure that it does. So . . . you're welcome."

Axel dropped his arm to my waist. He dipped me low to the ground and planted a light kiss on my lips. "No. *You're* welcome."

"For what, exactly?" I blinked up at him.

"For the absolutely unforgettable trip I'm about to take you on."

"Another trip?" I groaned as he guided me upright. "We just got back."

"True." Axel stared at the sky. "If I have to leave my parents stranded on that gods forsaken island while you and I lounge around Valkyris, I suppose they'll forgive us. Eventually."

My breath caught. "We get to bring your parents home!"

"Is that a yes on the boat trip?"

"*Boat* trip . . ." I tilted my head. "Are you going to do *any* of the rowing this time?"

Axel's eyes narrowed. "I told you. That was only because I was *injured.* I am normally an excellent sailor."

"That remains to be seen," I teased.

Axel growled. My breath hitched as he dipped me again. This time his kiss was slow, and deep, and completely and totally unforgettable.

I never wanted him to let go.

## CHAPTER 16

**T**ORSTEIN OFFERED TO PORT us straight to the island. He said he felt awful about stranding Axel's parents and wanted to make their return as easy as possible. But Axel wanted to do this on his own. I suspected a part of him wanted some time to process the enormity of seeing his family again. Since he'd only just come back from a mission, the two-day trip would give him the chance to decompress—to shift his mindset from assassin to civilian, if only for a short time.

I wasn't about to complain. I'd experienced enough portals in the past two months to last a lifetime. Besides, two days off-duty with Axel—even if we would be in choppy waters—sounded like a dream. It would be the longest chunk of alone time we'd had since we started dating. And while I knew Axel would be all kinds of nervous about seeing his parents for the first time in years, I was excited to be there to support him. We'd battled a dark mage, traveled through centuries, gone undercover, and fought portal-jumping monsters. It was about time we did something as simple as go on a date. Even a really unconventional one.

My heart was light as I climbed aboard the wooden ship with the red-and-white sails.

"Do you have the directions I wrote out?" Torstein asked.

"Right here." Axel held up the parchment.

"And the weapons I packed for you?" Janna chimed in.

"Under the bench." I pointed.

"And the blankets and pillows?" Brigga rested her cheek on Raynor's shoulder. "It's almost solstice—it's going to be really cold on the water."

"They're secured under a very helpful contraption Torstein magicked for us." I smiled. "Thanks for the rainproofing."

"It was the least I could do." Torstein shifted from one foot to the other. "Are you *sure* you don't want me to—"

"We want to go ourselves," Axel reiterated. "Don't worry. We'll be back in four days. Five, if the weather turns bad."

"You have all of the food rations we packed?" Freia tutted. "Including desserts?"

"We do," I assured. "I promise we'll feed the Anderssons a solid meal the moment we hit the shore."

"They may seem a bit . . . different," Halvar warned.

"There's no telling what years of isolation have done to them. But in time, all will be well. And I know that they've missed you every bit as much as Freia and I did while you were on your mission. Your parents are wonderful people, Axel. Two of the finest I've ever known. I cannot wait to see them again."

"Me too." Axel checked the sail. While he adjusted the fabric, I waved Torstein over.

"Come here," I whispered.

The light mage stepped to the dock's edge.

"This may be none of my business," I said quietly, "but in case you hadn't noticed, we currently live in a time *before* the mage war. *Before* Ama . . . well, you know. And I'm not sure what year she was born exactly, but—"

"She could very well be alive. The thought has crossed my mind," Torstein admitted. "Though I didn't meet her until well after the Viking Age, and even back then—er, in the future—it was . . . *is* considered rude to ask a woman the year she was born."

"But she could be out there somewhere," I said.

"I know." Longing colored Torstein's words. "I'm not entirely sure where she grew up—it was somewhere in the far north, but the land was so vast that she never was able to point it out on a map."

"Sounds like we have another tracking mission to look forward to." I grinned. "That is, if you want any help."

"I would be honored." Torstein bowed. "Now, go

right the wrong I committed. Please give the Anderssons my sincerest apologies."

"People with your abilities were manipulated and abused back then—er, now," I said gently. "Any one of us might have done the same. Besides, you left Axel's parents your home and your farmland. I'm sure they've made the best of it."

"All the same, I will apologize profusely when I see them again."

I reached out to clasp Torstein's hands. "I know you will."

"By the way, I've disposed of the ingredients," Torstein said.

I nodded. When we'd wrapped Sverrir's body, we'd discovered the items needed for the *Control* spell tucked inside his cloak. We'd actually come *that close* to being expunged from the historical record.

"Did you destroy all of them?" I asked.

"Except for the crystals—those I handed off to your chieftess. She promised to keep them secure."

"She's kept the dagger all these years," I said fondly. "She'll be able to look after them."

"I'm counting on it."

"Everything all right, Shieldmaiden?" Axel stepped over one of the benches.

"We're fine," I assured him. "Just getting some last-minute instructions from Valkyris' newest—and only —mage."

"How do you like it here so far?" Axel asked.

"It's different," Torstein admitted. "It's been a while

since I've lived in a time where indoor plumbing wasn't mainstream. Though I am impressed that you've managed to use *älva* dust to create your own version."

"We're resourceful like that." Axel slung his arm around my shoulder.

"So I'm learning." Torstein smiled. "Well, travel safely."

"Come home soon!" Janna stepped forward.

Freia waved. "Give your parents our love."

"Done. Done. And done." Axel glanced at the sky. "Guess we'd better shove off. The water's only going to get choppier."

"Great," I said weakly. My other seafaring experience had been that one awful boat trip. Axel had nearly irritated me to death, plus I'd been seasick the entire time. But my boyfriend had promised that I'd find my "sea legs" over the next few days. And, more importantly, Torstein had given me a bracelet that he swore would settle my stomach. He'd mumbled something about *the inner ear* and *pressure points*, though whether the bracelet affected those things using a potion or an enchantment, I had no idea. Either way, I was determined to pull my weight, support my boyfriend, and, gods willing, get over any seasickness *before* Axel's parents joined us on the boat. It was my very first family vacation.

And I intended to enjoy every minute of it.

To say the journey was rough would be an understatement. A storm blew in at the end of our first day at sea. While Torstein's magical rain shelter kept us dry, it couldn't stop the fierce winds from violently rocking the boat. My bracelet was put through its paces. And though I did eventually get sick, my stomach settled pretty quickly. In the morning, everything was smooth sailing—both inside the ship and at sea. By the time a landmass appeared on the horizon, I knew my churning gut had nothing to do with the waves. We were about to see Axel's parents.

I desperately wanted this to go well for him.

"You remember what Halvar said?" I asked nervously. "About them possibly seeming different from the way you knew them?"

"I do." Axel rowed steadily. "And I'm not concerned. Trauma may change people, but it doesn't alter their hearts. My parents are still in there somewhere. And I have the patience to wait them out."

I angled the sail so it caught the wind. "I know you do."

"Besides," Axel continued, "I've waited this long to see my parents again. I can hold out for a few extra weeks, months—whatever it takes."

I tied off the sail and sat down beside him. Then I leaned over to kiss his beard. "You're a remarkable man, Axel Andersson. You know that?"

"I do," he said amiably. "Now pick up an oar and row. There are no free rides on this ship."

"Please." I rolled my eyes. "I did *more* than my fair

share of rowing last time."

"You're never going to let that go, are you?"

"No." I picked up an oar and dug into the water.

"That's my girl."

I stuck out my tongue. "What will your parents say when they find out you grew up to be an insufferable know-it-all?"

"I have no idea." Axel shot me a wink. "But we're about to find out."

The boat drew up to the island. When we'd nearly reached the shore, we both jumped out and grabbed a rope. We waded through the surf, pulling the boat onto the sand before tying it to a nearby bush. When it was secure, I took a breath, looked around, and waited for Axel's instruction.

"This is your reunion," I said quietly. "Do you want to start searching, or would you rather give them time to find us before—"

"Hello?" an unseen man called. "You there! Are you injured? Do you need help?"

Axel's mouth opened, then closed. He seemed to be struggling to find his voice.

"Hello?" the man called again.

"We're not hurt," I offered back. "We've come to help you."

A long silence followed my declaration.

"Um . . . where exactly are you?" I shaded my eyes with one hand, and squinted into the brush. A handful of trees dotted the island but most of the foliage was low. I didn't see anyone standing within it.

"Axel," I whispered. "Where are they?"

Axel's mouth flapped again. Clearly, I'd be doing the talking.

"We can't see you," I yelled. "But we've brought food and clothing. We know you've been trapped here for quite some time. You must be hungry."

The man rose slowly from behind one of the bushes. He had the same emerald eyes, thick beard, and unruly, brown man-bun as Axel. But this Andersson's hair was streaked with grey. And his weather-worn skin looked as if it had aged slightly beyond his years. No doubt he'd been through Helheim and back, but he approached me with a cautious smile and an open hand. "You're not here to hurt us?"

"No." I shook my head. "We've come from Valkyris —Freia and Halvar sent us to bring you home. My name is Ingrid, and this . . . this is Axel."

My boyfriend shifted from one foot to the other.

The man turned his eyes to Axel. His voice was soft as he asked, "What did you say your name is?"

"I'm Axel." The words came on a soft breath. Axel stared at the man as if he were seeing him for the first time.

In a way, he was.

"Axel Andersson," the man said quietly. "Son of Arne and Astrid Andersson."

"Yes," Axel croaked.

The elder Andersson's eyes misted over. "I never thought I'd see you again."

"Neither did I." Axel's hands shook at his side. I

reached over and rested my fingertips on his arm. Mr. Andersson watched us closely. One corner of his mouth tugged up in a half-smile, and he called into the foliage.

"Astrid! Astrid, come out. It's Axel—he's here!"

A brown-haired woman walked cautiously across the sand. She stared at Axel as if he were a ghost. "Is it really you?"

"Mother," Axel whispered.

The woman reached out to touch Axel's cheek. He leaned into her hand, blinking rapidly. My heart tugged as a single tear slid into his beard. The woman's eyes crinkled around the corners. "I never thought I'd see you again."

"I know the feeling." Axel drew his shoulders back, took a steadying breath, and wrapped his arms around his mother. The woman's body shook as she folded herself into his embrace.

Mr. Andersson flung his arms around them both. They stood frozen in a hug while I did everything I could not to cry. The Anderssons looked so vulnerable —completely awed by the sight of the son they'd thought was lost to them forever. While Axel . . .

My breath hitched. Axel looked as if he'd just won a dozen Rufuses. As much as he'd made his dragons and his squadron his family, I knew that this moment meant everything to him. It was an honor to bear witness to it.

My heart swelled to near bursting as Axel pulled back, wiped his nose on the back of his sleeve, and offered me his snotty hand. I took it without hesitation.

"Mother, Father. I want to introduce you to Ingrid."

"You've taken a wife." Mrs. Andersson smiled approvingly. "Welcome to our family, Ingrid."

"Oh, no. I'm not his—"

"She looks strong." Mr. Andersson beamed. "You must be a warrior, Ingrid. Perhaps a shieldmaiden?"

"Yes, I am a shieldmaiden. But I'm not Axel's—"

"I've always wanted a daughter." Mrs. Andersson's grin lit up the entire island. "I do hope Axel's been treating you as well as we raised him to. Though I suppose we don't know how you were raised after we were marooned. Were you well cared for, son?"

"Halvar and Freia took me in," Axel said. "I was very well cared for, yes."

"I'm so glad. Oh, the years I spent worrying . . ." Mrs. Andersson wrung her fingers together.

"I was fine. I promise." Axel smiled at me. "And as for Ingrid, she and I are just—"

"Just perfect together," Mrs. Andersson trilled. "I can already tell."

I couldn't help but smile. Axel's parents were warm, and kind, and overflowing with love. They'd known me all of five minutes, and they'd already accepted me as a part of their family. If they wanted to believe Axel and I were . . . I nearly choked on the word. *Married*, well, then . . .

"Hey." Axel leaned in to whisper in my ear. "My

folks have spent years stranded on a deserted island. Do you *really* want to break their hearts right now?"

"Well, no. But . . ."

"We have a long boat ride—we can tell them tomorrow. Besides, I love you. It's only a matter of time. Right?"

My pulse quickened. It was the first time he'd ever told me he loved me. Not to mention . . .

*It's only a matter of time?*

Was he saying that he wanted . . . that we were . . . was that his way of . . .?

"Your mouth is doing that flapping fish thing." Axel touched one finger to my lips.

"Shut up, Axel," I hissed. "You did it earlier."

"Maybe." He traced my bottom lip with his thumb. "But I bet I wasn't as cute as you."

"You never are." I shot him my most intense glare, then treated his parents to a beatific smile. "Mr. and Mrs. Andersson, you must be starving. Freia sent us with a multi-course meal. She says she can't wait to cook for you once we bring you back to Valkyris, but she wanted to make sure you had a taste of home first. Once Axel and I unload the boat, we can eat."

"I'll help you." Axel's mom followed us across the sand. After a few steps, she stopped and turned to Axel. "I'm so happy you found such a wonderful bride, son."

"I'm not his—"

"I like her too," Axel said. "She's the only girl I've ever met who's fiercer than I am."

It was the best compliment he could have given me.

"Then you'd better hold onto her." Mr. Andersson looked fondly at his wife. "A strong partner will see you through a lifetime of adventures."

"Including a multi-year stay on a deserted island." Mrs. Andersson smiled back. "There's nobody I'd have rather been stranded with."

"And there's nobody I'd rather *finally* go home with." Mr. Andersson chuckled. "Right after a good meal, of course."

*Of course.*

We spent the next few hours eating, laughing, and catching up on a decade of stories. When we finally pushed the boat away from the island, Axel tossed his parents a blanket, adjusted the sail, and slung his arm around my shoulders.

"Ready to go home?" he asked. "Maybe catch a little bit of downtime before *our* next big adventure?"

"Absolutely." I looked up at him. "But why do I have the feeling that life with you will consist of very little downtime?"

"Because, Shieldmaiden, I am nothing short of thrilling." Axel kissed the top of my head. "And you wouldn't want me any other way."

"No." I nestled my cheek against his chest. "I suppose I wouldn't."

As we entered the open ocean, we picked up speed. It would be smooth sailing for the rest of our trip. And after that, well . . . Axel and I had a lifetime of adventures to look forward to.

I couldn't wait to discover them all.

# SHIELDMAIDEN SQUADRON'S LEFSE RECIPE

## (INSTANT POTATO VERSION)

7 oz instant potato flakes
1 tbsp melted butter
1 cup boiling water
2 tsp salt
1 cup whole milk
1.5 – 2 cups of flour

Combine potato flakes and salt. Combine water, milk and butter. Mix together, then add flour until dough is soft but not sticky. Separate into logs, cover with a cloth, and refrigerate overnight.

The next day: Divide logs into small lefse balls, and roll to desired thickness. Cook both sides in a pan on high heat. Serve with butter, cinnamon and sugar. (Or Nutella!)

Take a picture and share it with me!
Social links at www.stbende.com.

**Meet the rest of the Valkyris crew in**
**VIKING ACADEMY**

*Erik held me until my shoulders stopped shaking—whether it was a minute or an hour, I couldn't tell. The only things I knew for sure were:*

1. *I was trapped a thousand years in the past, with little hope of ever going home. And,*
2. *I was wrapped in the arms of the most absurdly gorgeous Viking to have ever walked the face of the Earth.*

*Maybe my old life was overrated.*

When seventeen-year-old Saga Skånstad discovers an antique dagger, she's instantly sucked into a world where Vikings rule the seas and dragons roam the skies, and the only thing more dangerous than the chief who takes her captive is the rival who steals her away. The heir of Norway's most feared tribe is fierce, cold, and absolutely unyielding. With intruders encroaching upon his borders, Erik Halvarsson has little patience for the girl whose ignorance threatens his very existence. He enlists Saga in the magical Valkyris Academy, where she learns the skills she'll need to protect herself from foreign raiders and domestic terrors. But nothing can protect her from falling for the one guy in all the world she's absolutely forbidden to choose . . . or from risking everything to unlock the secrets that haunt him.

When darkness threatens Saga's new home, she must decide whether to return to the life she's always known, or fight for a love she never could have imagined. Her decision will determine a legacy—not only for Saga, but for the world she never knew she was fated to lead.

**Meet Axel Andersson's not-so-mythical Asgardian relative in ...**

**THE ÆRE SAGA: PERFEKT ORDER**

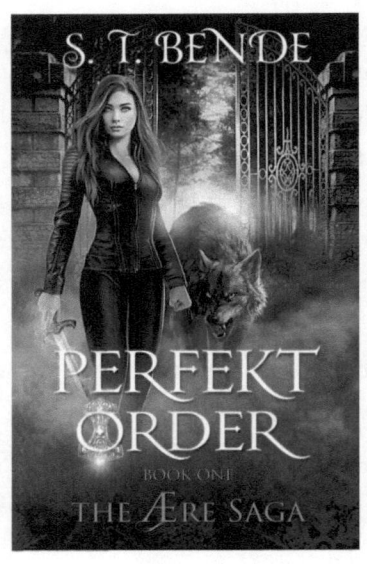

All's fair when you're in love with War.

For seventeen-year-old Mia Ahlström, a world ruled by order is the only world she allows. A lifetime of chore charts, to-do lists and study schedules have helped earn her a spot at Redwood State University's engineering program. And while her five year plan includes finding her very own happily-evah-aftah, years at an all-girls boarding school left her feeling woefully unprepared for keg parties and co-ed extracurricular activities.

So nothing surprises her more than catching the eye of Tyr Fredriksen at her first college party. The imposing Swede is arrogantly charming, stubbornly overprotective, and runs hot-and-cold in ways that defy reason... until Mia learns that she's fallen for the Norse God of War; an immortal battle deity hiding on Midgard (Earth) to protect a valuable Asgardian treasure from a feral enemy. With a price on his head, Tyr brings more than a little excitement to Mia's rigidly controlled life. Choosing Tyr may be the biggest distraction—or the greatest adventure—she's ever had.

## ACKNOWLEDGMENTS

To my adventurous little family—you are my heart. I am so grateful God gave me you.

To Lauren Clarke at CREATING ink, who's been with me since day one—and who is the epitome of kindness, patience, and wisdom. To Mariana, for being all the things, always—and for doing so with remarkable grace. And to Alison, who championed Ingrid's happily ever after from her very first appearance in Viking Academy. Thank you for your friendship.

To the readers who dream across the realms with me—thank you for seeing the world through magic-tinted glasses. To everyone who has the spirit of a shieldmaiden—thank you for sharing your light with our world. And to MorMorMa. Always.

# ABOUT THE AUTHOR

Before finding domestic bliss in suburbia, S.T. Bende lived in Manhattan Beach (where she became overly fond of Peet's Coffee) and studied Shakespeare in Europe... where she became overly fond of McVitie's cookies.

S.T.'s love of Scandinavian culture, and a very patient Norwegian teacher, inspired her YA Norse fantasy series'. And her deep love of a galaxy far, far away led to her writing children's books for the Star Wars franchise. As an experienced IP writer, she's written multiple books published by Disney-Lucasfilm Press and its licensees.

When she's not creating stories, S.T. dreams of skiing on Jotunheim and Hoth.

Learn more about the world of S.T. Bende
at www.stbende.com .